Mine to Save

Pine Ridge Pack: Book 1

Jayda Marx

Author's Note

Thank you for your interest in my book! This paranormal romance features my take on some seriously sexy wolf shifters. They share many attributes of shifters found in other fictional works, but not all. This book contains fated mates, sweet moments and lots of laughs. My stories are low angst and **insta-love.** They follow **relationships on the fast track**, and I live for sweetness! I want my readers to finish my books with a smile on their face and a fierce case of the warm and fuzzies. Laughter is guaranteed, and each read delivers its own type of drama. Thanks again for taking a look and happy reading!

Chapter One

Rory

I sat in a booth at my favorite pizza place waiting for my friend to arrive, drumming my fingers on the box of my new purchase. I couldn't wait to show Dax; I'd been talking about buying this camera for months. I *loved* photography, but there was only so much I could do with the camera app on my phone. So, I saved every dollar I could from my grocery store job to finally buy a nice Nikon. It wasn't top of the line, but to me, it was incredible.

My attention was caught by Dax sitting down across from me. He huffed as he looked at his stomach, which pressed into the tabletop. "I think this might be my wake-up call." I snorted a laugh and shook my

"How is Justin?" I asked, trying not to gag when I said his name. "Has he found a job yet?"

"No, the poor guy isn't having very good luck. It's all that window manufacturer's fault. I still don't understand why they fired him."

I blinked in disbelief. The factory fired Justin because he threw a temper tantrum and put his fist through a plate glass window. He had a nasty temper, which is another reason why I hated him. But, he'd never physically harmed Dax, and every time I tried to talk to my friend about my concerns, it ended up in a fight between us, so I'd learned to hold my tongue.

"But it's okay," Dax shrugged. "I've got an interview this afternoon at the movie theater. I figured I could pick up some afternoon and evening hours to help cover the bills."

"You're going to take a second job?" Dax already worked nights cleaning office buildings. Adding even more hours would cut into his sleep.

"Only until Justin finds work. I'm sure it won't be long." I didn't believe it for a minute; if Dax was covering expenses, Justin would take the opportunity to sit on his lazy ass and mooch off of my friend, but I again kept my thoughts to myself.

"What should we get to eat?" I asked, changing the subject. I didn't want to spend another minute on Justin.

"Well, I'm *supposed* to be on a diet, so I guess I'll just get a salad or something."

"*Or*, we could split an order of cheese fries and a pepperoni pizza."

"I like the way you think," he grinned. "But if Justin asks, I got a salad."

I had a better idea; if Justin asked, I'd punch him right in the face. I mentally rolled my eyes at myself; I was a relatively short, scrawny nerd with glasses. I was intimidating to exactly no one.

Our waitress came by to take our order and delivered our drinks. When we were alone again, I turned my attention back to my friend.

"Wait a minute; if you've got an interview this afternoon, you won't be able to come to the state forest with me. I was planning on hiking some trails and getting lots of pictures with this." I hefted the box onto the table and Dax's eyes widened.

"Ooh, you got it? Let me see!" He grabbed the box and read over the details printed on the side. "This is awesome, Roar. You've been wanting this thing forever. I'm happy for you."

"Thanks," I smiled. I was bummed Dax had plans already; I really wanted to try my camera out, but I didn't want to go alone. "When will you be free so we can plan a trip out to the forest?"

"I honestly have no clue," he shrugged. "Especially if I get this second job; my hours will probably be all over the place. But you shouldn't wait for me; you had plans of going today, so you should go. You can show me all the great pictures you get next time we hang out."

"I'm afraid I'll get lost or something," I admitted. I had a terrible sense of direction, so wandering around the woods alone didn't sound like the smartest idea.

"Just stay on the paths and you'll be fine. They're all marked. Or so I've heard anyway; obviously my fat ass hasn't been hiking many trails lately."

"Come on, don't say stuff like that," I begged.

"Sorry," he replied with a tight smile. He knew I hated it when he talked badly about himself. "I meant to say that I'm in such peak physical condition, trail hiking is just too easy for me. I limit myself to marathon runs and bench-pressing tractors."

I snorted. "That's better." I let out a long breath. "Okay, I think I *will* go; the fall colors on the trees are gorgeous right now. I want to capture them before a big rain comes through and knocks them all down." We usually only had a window of a couple of weeks that the trees were pretty, and I didn't want to miss them.

"Awesome. I can't wait to see what you get. Just do me a favor and call me when you get back into town, okay? I'm sure you'll be fine, but now you've put images of you wandering around lost in the woods into my head."

I smiled; Dax and I always looked out for one another and took care of each other. "I promise."

Chapter Two

Phoenix

"This is my favorite time of year," Rowan said as he came onto the porch of my cabin and sat in the patio chair beside me.

"Mine too," I smiled. The air was crisp and clean, and the foliage was beautiful within the depths of the state park where Rowan, Stone and I lived. We had an agreement with the state government; they knew of our identity and we were protected within the area. They also provided us with a small plot of land along the outskirts of the forest (along with a decent paycheck) in exchange for our services in protecting and monitoring the area. The three of us could roam the lands quickly and efficiently and were able to explore areas humans couldn't access. It was a perfect job for three wolf shifters.

Our pack of three was small but mighty. I trusted Rowan and Stone with my life, and I had their trust in return; it was imperative as their alpha to lead with honor and integrity. The three of us had been together since we were born. We were raised as members of the Silver Birch Pack, under the lead of my father, Alpha Dean. We became fast friends and formed lasting bonds. From a very young age, we knew that as an alpha, I would one day leave my father's pack to lead my own. Even as children, Stone and Rowan swore their allegiance to me and vowed to follow me when I left. However, we never could have envisioned the events that led up to our departure.

My brother Raven was also born an alpha; he had the call to lead along with inherent strength. Unfortunately, he lacked morality. He was greedy and callus. Instead of fulfilling his destiny and forging his own path, he challenged our father to a fight to the death for his rule over his pack. My father loved my brother and refused to fight his own son. He offered himself up for slaughter; standing still as Raven struck our father down. Since our mother was our father's true and bonded soulmate, her life was also cut short. That day, I lost my entire family since I no longer claimed my brother.

That night, Rowan, Stone and I fled. I couldn't stand being under my brother's rule. Even though I hated him, I also couldn't bring myself to fight him. Plus, I was too distraught over the loss of my parents to perform my best. Even if I could, my friends would not have let me fight Raven alone, and I wouldn't risk their lives against my wicked brother and his friends.

It took several years of travelling for us to finally find our place in the world. Now we formed the Pine Ridge Pack. We were settled in the forest, living in three small cabins built by our own hands. Raven's pack continued to dwindle. Over the last decade, I heard of many members fleeing to join other packs not ruled by greed and fear. The only members he had left were those as bloodthirsty and corrupt as he was. My pack was few in number, but I would rather have two men I trusted than a hundred who may stab me in the back.

My thoughts were interrupted by Rowan's happy sigh as he stretched out his legs and folded his hands behind his head. I opened the cooler by my opposite side and retrieved a bottle, which I offered to my friend. "Beer?"

"Thanks." Rowan took the bottle with a smile, popped the cap and took a long swig. As shifters, our tolerance was high, but it was always nice to kick back and relax with a drink.

Just then, a rustling along the tree line caught my attention. I grinned at the sight of a large gray wolf stalking out of the woods. It stretched its front paws low to the ground and hoisted its ass up in the air. Within moments, its hair retreated, and its bones snapped and reformed. Its snout shrank and its ears lowered. The animal reared up on its hind legs and in a blink, transformed into my friend Stone. The shifting process *looked* painful but felt like a good stretch after waking.

Stone popped his neck from side to side as he approached my cabin. Looking at him, one might assume *he* was the alpha of our pack. Rowan and I were both tall and muscular, as most shifters were, but Stone was built like a brick wall. His muscles bulged and rippled with the slightest movement. He also kept his head shaved to could catalog every scent they encountered, but I was drawing a blank on this one.

"Hey, did you change your soap or something?" I asked, leaning closer to Stone and inhaling deeply. The scent was too faint to catch again. He must have been close to the flower but not touched it.

"No and stop sniffing me; it's fuckin' weird." He put his hand on my forehead and pushed me away. Rowan chuckled as I shot an irritated look at Stone. I finally shrugged and went back to my beer. The next time I went out in the woods, I'd search for the elusive flower.

Stone finished his beer and chucked the empty bottle into the small recycling bin tucked into the corner of my porch. He belched loudly and scratched his stomach. "It doesn't get much better than this, does it?" he asked, looking at the bright fall colors around us.

"I don't know," Rowan said on a sigh. "Having my mate on my lap would definitely help."

"Oh god, here we go again," Stone groaned with an eye roll. It wasn't the first time we'd heard Rowan talk about a mate; the man was obsessed with finding his fated match. Every shifter had one true soulmate granted to them by Fate; one person they were to love, protect and cherish for all time, though none of us knew when we'd meet ours.

Rowan dreamed of that day often and wasn't shy about it. His icy blue eyes got a dreamy faraway look whenever he discussed finding his future mate. Whoever ended up being Rowan's match would be one lucky bastard; as gruff and intimidating as Stone was, that's how tenderhearted and romantic Rowan was. His exterior was strong and formidable, but his insides were goo. He'd

Stone, are you up for a visit to the city tonight?"

"Hell yeah," he answered with a wicked smile.

"Great," Rowan replied. "Just give me a few minutes to get presentable. If I *do* meet my mate tonight, I want to look my best."

"Guess I'll slap on some clothes too," Stone shrugged. "Although if I showed up like this, I could get to the fun faster." Men already clamored all over themselves to get to him; I couldn't imagine what the mob would look like if he showed up shirtless.

"Well good luck to both of you," I offered. Tonight was my rotation to go into the forest and check the trails for lost tourists, fire hazards and fallen limbs or anything else blocking the paths.

heart raced in my chest. My blood pumped feverishly through my veins. An uncontrollable whimper of longing left my mouth. It was then that I realized I wasn't tracking some*thing*, but some*one*. I'd been following the pheromones of my mate.

My mind spun. *My mate was here!* With how strong the scent was, he was here today; maybe within the past few hours. I knew my mate was a male; not only was that my preference, but I could smell it. My mate was male and human. I pawed at the ground as thoughts raced through my brain. *Who is he? Where is he? How will I ever find him again? Will he come back? How am I supposed to live without him until I locate him?*

I paced back and forth, trying to settle my troubled mind. And then I saw it. My heart sank as I noticed a board that made up the guard rail along the cliffside was snapped in two. I instinctively knew something was wrong. I walked to the edge of the cliff and strained my neck to peer over the side. Though it was pitch black outside, I could make out an outline of a small body crumpled onto the rocks. *Please god, no.*

I sprinted along the rail and leapt over the board onto an area of the cliffside that sloped down at a more gradual angle; still too steep for human legs, but my wolf could handle it. I slid and tumbled down the dirt until I reached the rocky bottom. I jumped over a few large boulders until I was only feet away from my mate. His delicious scent permeated the air, but I couldn't enjoy it. I was too worried about his welfare.

I stalked over to his body, trying to keep my hopes down and prepare myself for the worst. When I was next to him, my breath caught. He was beautiful. His black hair was shiny and combed back away from his face. His features were delicate, and his milky skin was smooth. Circular black framed glasses were askew over his nose from the fall. His body was a little on the short side and very thin. He'd need my protection. *If I'm not already too late.* My heart ached at the thought, and at the fact that I wasn't here when he needed me. Who knows how long I'd left him lying here alone?

I licked his smooth cheeks, trying to rouse him. I whimpered when he didn't budge. Just as I was about to shift into my human form to check for a pulse, my mate's eyes slowly peeled open. They were a beautiful shade of chocolate brown, but I was concerned by the way his pupils were constricted into small points. *But he's alive.* Hope bloomed inside my chest.

"Hello, pretty wolf," my mate whispered. His voice was quiet and strained, but still the most beautiful sound I'd ever heard. He obviously wasn't in his right mind, though; nobody would speak to a wolf as if they were greeting an old friend. I worried before he got hurt. If I'd been the one to check out the noise, I could have kept any of this from happening.

"Jesus, is he okay? He fell almost thirty feet!" Rowan exclaimed, dropping to his knees and placing his hands on my mate's chest. I couldn't stop the growl that rumbled from me. Rowan recoiled his arms and stared at me with wide eyes.

"Sorry," I offered, shaking my head. I'd never snap at my friend on purpose. "The sight of you naked with your hands on him was just too much." Stone and Rowan both still looked confused. "He's my mate."

A slow smile spread over Rowan's face. "Your *mate*? Phoenix, this is incredible. Congratulations!"

"Maybe we should save that for *after* we've made sure he doesn't die on this rock," Stone said. I growled at him too, but he just rolled his eyes. "I'm not being a dick; I'm saying let's get him out of here."

"Right, sorry," I replied, but Stone just waved me off. "But *how* do we get him out of here? We can't make it up the hillside in human form, but we can't carry him in wolf form."

"I've got rope at my place," Stone answered. "We can rig up something to pull him back up over the cliff face." He was a great critical thinker and didn't allow emotions to interfere.

"I'll stay here with Phoenix and look over his mate," Rowan added. Stone nodded and, in a blink, he shifted into wolf form and raced back up the hillside.

"I'll have to touch him to check him out," Rowan said gently. "Is that okay?" I nodded. Rowan spent a lot of time with the healer of our last pack and learned a lot. He knew how to check for broken bones and set

"May I lift his shirt?" Rowan asked, and I nodded. I appreciated his courtesy and concern; mates were the most precious and loved possession of any shifter. We were fiercely loyal and protective of them. Disrespect to a shifter's mate or the bond shared between them was cause for expulsion from the pack. Even though I'd known Rowan all of my life and loved him like a brother, my loyalty lay with my mate from now on. I wouldn't think twice about rejecting anyone who disrespected him, or killing anyone who harmed him.

Rowan raised my mate's shirt and my heart raced at the sight of his smooth, creamy skin. His body was taut and slim, and I could make out the impressions of his last few ribs. Rowan pressed his fingers gently down my mate's sides before looking at me. "I don't feel any broken bones here either, and there's no massive bruising or other signs of internal bleeding. I'm sure he's bruised his ribs, though, and possibly jarred his back. He's lucky he landed on his side; if he'd hit his spine, he could have done serious damage. Though nothing's broken, when he wakes up, he will be in significant pain." He lowered his shirt. "Plus, he's been exposed to this cold weather and wind in such thin clothing. He doesn't have much body fat, so I'm worried he'll soon suffer effects of hypothermia if he isn't already. Has he been shivering at all?"

"Yes. I was lying on top of him earlier to try to keep him warm. Oh god, you don't think I hurt his ribs worse do you?"

"I think what's most important right now is keeping him warm. His body can't heal itself if it's also trying to raise his body temperature. When we get him to your cabin, I recommend skin-to-skin contact and lots of blankets. Your body heat will help raise his core temperature. Plus, cuddling can reduce anxiety and help strengthen his immune system, so you will be helping him to relax and heal."

I certainly had no issues cuddling with my mate; the very thought made my pulse race and my blood burn. There was just one problem. "He said he loves someone else," I told my friend sadly. "Before he passed out."

Rowan gave me a sad smile and placed his hand on my shoulder. "Mates trump all. If he thinks he is in love with someone else, he is mistaken. Once he meets you and spends time with you, he will see you're the one he's meant to be with." I gave him a nod of thanks. "Give me your hands." I did as Rowan asked, and he placed my palms on my mate's chest. "Rub against his trunk to warm him until we can get him out of here."

I massaged gentle circles over his chest and stomach, being careful not to press too firmly and risk hurting him. Rowan patted my shoulder and gave me an easy smile. "I'm very happy for you, Alpha. May I ask what it was like when you found him and realized he was yours?"

I smiled back at my friend, not surprised he wanted details. "It was incredible. I scented him nearly two miles away. At first I couldn't place the smell; just that it was wonderful. I needed more; my body craved it. I *needed* to get to the source. It wasn't until I got closer that I realized I was tracking my mate's pheromones, and that it was his body calling out to me. When I saw he was injured, my heart shattered at the thought of losing him. You know now that I've met my fated mate, I can never have another man. I will never want another. I couldn't stop thinking of an eternal life alone, missing and pining over a mate I never got to meet."

Rowan whimpered his sadness. I wanted to console him, but also didn't want

I'd ever seen, smiling widely at the camera with pearly white teeth and sparkling eyes. I read the rest of the information on the card to myself, learning my mate was twenty two, five foot seven, 138 pounds and that he lived in an apartment downtown. I slipped his wallet back into his pocket and Rowan rolled him back onto his spine. I immediately returned to rubbing his torso to warm him.

"Rory," Rowan repeated with a smile on his face. "I like it. I've never known anyone with that name."

"Me neither." My mate was one of a kind.

Just then, a whistle from overhead caught our attention. Stone was looking over the edge of the cliff. "Heads up; I'm lowering the rope! Make sure he's tied up securely. Tell me when you're ready and I'll pull him up."

A long, thick white rope cascaded over the rocks and fell with a *thud* beside me. Rowan and I worked together to quickly secure Rory with the cord. We tied strong bowline knots around his ankles, midsection and shoulders, creating a sling to cradle his body.

"I'll go halfway up the hill to watch for any issues while Stone pulls him up," Rowan offered. Stone was plenty strong enough to hoist my small mate up the cliffside by himself.

"Good idea. I'll stay down here to catch him in case he falls." Our knots were sturdy, but I wasn't taking any chances. Rowan shifted and ran about halfway up the incline, steadying himself in the dirt. "Okay, Stone!"

I watched with bated breath as Rory rose a few inches from the ground as Stone pulled the rope. My mate rose swiftly and steadily, only rocking side to side a little as he ascended. As soon as his body disappeared over the top of the cliff, I shifted and darted up the hillside after Rowan.

I made it to Rory's side just as Stone untied the last knot. I shifted back into human form and scooped his limp body into my arms and held him close. Since he was unable to hold onto me, I positioned him in my hold bridal style. He was heaven in my arms. My two friends took off in wolf form toward our cabins. I knew they'd prepare my home for my arrival with my mate.

I dashed back down the trail as fast as I could without jostling Rory. Rocks and twigs along the path cut my feet as I ran, but each nick healed quickly. I didn't stop to collect the clothes I shed earlier. I'd get them tomorrow, or never. I really didn't care. The most important thing was getting my mate to my cabin and getting him warm and comfortable.

My breath caught when my mate's eyes opened. He moaned and scrunched up his brow in pain. "It's okay, Rory. I've got you," I soothed, quickening my pace. "We're almost home."

He only mumbled "Pretty eyes," before closing his again, but it was enough to make my heart race. He'd noticed me, even if only briefly, and liked what he saw. Though his instincts wouldn't be as strong as mine as a shifter, he would still feel a draw to me. His attraction would grow until his blood burned and an animalistic heat took over his body until our bond was complete. It was Fate's way of ensuring a quick and solid match. I knew it would cause poor Rory confusion because of his relationship with another man, but I could never let him go. He was my one and only love for my eternal life. Once bonded as my mate, Rory would receive immortality as well, as I could never live without him.

I ran faster when my cabin came into view. I leapt onto the porch, where my friends waited, dressed in low-slung sweatpants. They'd covered themselves in case my mate woke on our journey, but unfortunately, he was unconscious again. I entered my home and my heart swelled at the sight of a roaring fire in my fireplace. When I entered my bedroom, I noticed that my bed was piled high with every blanket from not only my own house, but also every one from my friends'.

"Thank you," I told them both seriously as I cradled Rory closer to my chest. Stone just nodded his head, and Rowan gave me a wide smile.

"Of course. We'll leave you now to tend to your mate." Since he'd recommended skin-to-skin contact, they were leaving so they wouldn't see Rory undressed. I wouldn't be able to handle other men being around my mate when his body wasn't covered. Shifters were extremely territorial, and I'd never want to hurt my friends. "Call for us if you need *anything*," he added once they reached the door. Stone waved over his head and closed the door behind them as they left my cabin.

I pulled down the mountain of blankets and gently laid Rory onto my mattress. I removed each of his shoes and socks, revealing his cute little feet. Not that they were tiny, but they were small compared to my size thirteens. I took a deep breath and unbuttoned his jeans. I averted my eyes from the soft lump in his briefs as I pulled the denim down his legs. I didn't want to take advantage of my mate's injury.

I took his glasses from his face, noticing the frames were bent from his fall. I manipulated them in my hands until they were straight again and folded them on my nightstand. The last thing I removed was Rory's shirt. I was extra gentle so that I didn't disturb his rib injuries. Once he was only in a pair of gray briefs, I went to my dresser and pulled on a pair of boxers. It would be startling enough for my mate when he woke up in a strange bed next to me; I wouldn't allow myself to be completely naked with him.

I laid down beside him in bed and covered us up with the quilts, making sure they were tucked closely around Rory. I covered every inch of his body all the way up to his chin before nestling in close to him. I folded my arm across his stomach and tangled my legs around his, touching as much of my skin to his as possible and ignoring how wonderful he felt against me. This wasn't the time to relish his soft skin and breathe in his intoxicating scent; it was the time to provide him comfort and care.

It was like a furnace beneath all of the blankets plus the heat from the fire. I immediately began to sweat, but I didn't care. I'd do anything to help my mate. I held him close to me, whispering words of love and comfort into his ear, praying he woke up soon.

Chapter Four

Rory

I slowly awoke and cringed at the pain in my head and shooting down my side. *Why am I hurting like this?* I searched my scrambled brain for clues and remembered my fall. *Okay, well, I guess I didn't die; that's good. And I wasn't eaten; even better.* I tried to hoist myself up into a sitting position, but cried out at the pain in my ribs.

"Easy, sweetheart," a voice crooned beside me. "Just relax, I've got you." The voice soothed something deep inside me. I settled back down onto what I realized was a pillow beneath my head, nestling into the soft mattress below me. "There you go, Rory. I'm right here." An arm tightened its hold around me and I snuggled against the warm body that lay beside me, ready to go back to sleep.

My eyes popped open. *An arm is around me. A body is next to me. I don't know that voice. I'm in a bed that's not mine.* Fear pulled me from my relaxed state and I jumped from the bed onto the floor. Pain burst through my head and I yelled out, falling to my knees; my *bare* knees. *Where are my clothes?*

My stomach twisted and churned as I swayed on the spot. I looked around and found a small trash can in the corner of the room. I was luckily able to reach it just in time to vomit into it. As I heaved, the pain in my side intensified and tears poured down my face.

"It's okay, sweetheart," the man soothed as he too emerged from the bed. He stepped behind me and squatted down to place his large hand on my back as I threw up. I still hadn't seen him. His voice and actions spoke comfort, but I was still scared out of my mind to wake up like this with a stranger.

"Please don't touch me," I begged when I had nothing left to vomit up. I curled my arms around the trash can and folded my body in, fighting against my pain as I tried to make myself smaller.

"I'm sorry, Rory; am I hurting you?"

"I don't know you!" I yelled too loudly, causing a burst of discomfort in my head. "I don't know what's going on! I woke up in a random man's bed in my underwear. What did you do to me?" The man made a noise that sounded like a wounded puppy. My heart clenched and my dumb self nearly apologized until I remembered my predicament.

The man stood up behind me and I heard him take a few heavy steps away. The mattress squeaked as he sat down on it. I was thankful for the distance but missed his presence at the same time.

"I didn't do anything to you, I swear it," he replied softly, still sounding hurt. "I found you at the bottom of the cliff after seeing the broken guardrail. My friends and I rescued you and I brought you home with me. I live within the state forest, so my cabin was close. You have a concussion and bruised ribs, and you were also going into hypothermia from being in the cold weather so long. My friend has medical training and suggested skin-to-skin contact to bring your body temperature up. I undressed you to your underwear so that my skin could touch yours, but I promise I did not touch any of your private areas. I was only trying to help. I'm sorry if I offended you."

Shit. The man saved me from certain death and the first thing I do is accuse him of something terrible. "No, I'm sorry," I replied in a whisper, drying my eyes. "I shouldn't have said that; I was just frightened."

"I understand. You had a bad fall and woke up in a strange place with a strange man. Please don't apologize, Rory."

"How do you know my name?" As I asked, I pushed the trash can away from me. The smell of my vomit was making me sick again.

"I checked your ID."

Makes sense. "And what's your name?"

"My name is Phoenix and you're in my cabin. We're near the Pine Ridge Trail of the state forest. It's about four miles from where you fell."

"Thank you." I appreciated the information; it was helping me get my bearings and piece together what happened.

I gripped the edge of the nightstand to support myself as I stood, and my fingers brushed against the frames of my glasses. I put them on, stood on shaky legs, and turned to face Phoenix. When my gaze landed on him for the first time, my jaw dropped. He was stunning. Even though he was sitting down, I could tell he was tall. His body was smooth, toned and muscular. On his chest was a sexy tribal tattoo of a wolf howling. His sharp jaw was covered in brown scruff that matched his short, messy hair, and he had the most mesmerizing emerald eyes I'd ever seen. *Wait, I've seen them before.* "Pretty eyes," I whispered, and Phoenix grinned from ear to ear. "I remember them."

"You woke up briefly when I was carrying you here."

"You carried me for four miles?" I asked, dumbfounded. I doubted I could even *walk* four miles without needing an oxygen tank.

"Of course," he shrugged like it wasn't a big deal. "You needed help."

"Wow." I shook my head, but hissed at the pain it caused.

"Please sit down," he requested, jumping from the bed. He propped a few pillows on top of each other against the headboard and folded down the many blankets on his bed. "You need to rest." I sat on the mattress and leaned against the pillows, and Phoenix was quick to tuck the blankets around my body. "Are you warm enough?"

"Yes, thank you." I looked into his sparkling eyes and gave the best smile I could muster with the pain I felt. "And thank you for saving me. I would've been a goner without you."

"It's my pleasure." He reached his hand out to stroke my cheek, but stopped within an inch of touching me.

"It's okay," I whispered, and he smiled before trailing the backs of his fingers along my smooth skin. His touch was soothing. I'd known this man for mere minutes but something about having him close to me made me feel complete. Maybe I was still suffering from a brain injury, but I was comfortable around him. Hell, if he wanted to hurt me, he'd have done it when I was unconscious. Plus, having an insanely hot man tending to me wasn't the worst fate in the world.

"Is there anything I can get for you?"

"Do you have any Tylenol? I could really use something for this pain."

Phoenix's face scrunched up. "I'm sorry, but I don't have any medicine here." It seemed odd to not even have Tylenol, but also, he looked like a really healthy guy. A really fit guy. A really hot guy. I blinked away the thoughts; Phoenix was being so kind to take care of me. The last thing he needed was a scrawny nerd ogling him and making him uncomfortable. "But I'll call my friend Rowan; he'll have something to help."

"Is he the doctor?" He mentioned one of his friends had medical training.

Phoenix bounced his head left to right. "Of sorts." *Well that's reassuring.* I wondered what kind of back alley pills I was about to ingest. Hell, I didn't care. I'd swallow them and be thankful without asking questions. *Anything* to help this pain. Phoenix crossed the room and picked up a phone from its receiver. He dialed a number and soon spoke to a person on the other line.

"He's awake. Would you mind coming over to check him out again? He threw up a while ago." Phoenix was silent as his friend spoke. "Also, he's in a lot of pain. Do you have anything to help him?" More silence. "Great. Thank you, Rowan. I'll see you soon."

Phoenix hung up and walked back over to the bed. He pointed to the mattress and raised his brows in question. I scooted my legs over so he could sit down next to me. He patted my knee and I nearly sighed at the contact. "Rowan will be here shortly. He said nausea and vomiting are side effects of the concussion, but he'll bring you something for that and the pain. He lives next door, so it will be only a few minutes."

"That's amazing, thank you." I let out a long breath of relief, knowing help was on the way.

"Maybe we should get your clothes back on," Phoenix suggested, already bending down to pick up my pants from the floor.

"Doesn't he want to check my ribs? It'll be easier if I stay like this. I don't mind; all the important bits are covered."

Phoenix's jaw clenched as he swallowed. "Yes, I suppose it will be easier." It sounded like he had to choke out the words. I was sure I was imagining things, but it was almost like he was jealous over me; like he didn't want his friend to see me. That was crazy, though. I was nothing special, and certainly nothing to be jealous over.

Talking about Phoenix's friend brought a thought to the forefront of my mind and worry bolted through me. "Oh god, what time is it?"

Phoenix looked at the nightstand and back at me. "A little after ten."

"At night?"

"No, the morning. You slept for at least twelve hours. I didn't want to wake you; you needed the rest."

"Oh shit. Oh shit, shit, shit."

Phoenix's pretty eyes grew wide. "What is it? Is something wrong?"

"Dax is going to kill me. He's probably worried sick. I promised I'd call him when I got home yesterday evening but then, you know, tried to die. Is my phone here? Did it survive?" I sat up and was again hit with a shot of blinding pain. I moaned and grabbed my forehead.

"Shh, it's okay," Phoenix soothed, his voice sounding distant and sad. "Yes, your phone is fine; it was in your front pocket and didn't hit the ground. But you won't get reception here. You can use my landline to call Dax. You relax and I'll grab it for you." He stood and crossed the room with slumped shoulders. He retrieved the phone and handed it to me with a sad smile. "Is Dax your boyfriend or your..." he swallowed hard before asking, "Husband?" I narrowed my eyes in confusion. "You were in and out of it last night; you said you wished you could tell Dax you loved him."

Either I was nuts or Phoenix sounded upset that I was with someone. Either way, I wanted to console him. I didn't understand it, but the sight of him upset hurt almost as badly as my scrambled brain. "No, nothing like that. Dax has been my best friend for as long as I can remember. I love him like a brother; he's my family."

"Oh." A huge smile took over his pouty lips. "I'm really glad to hear that."

He is? Okay, maybe I'm not so nuts after all. He's gotta be, though. There's no logical reason he should be this happy. Oh god; maybe he is nuts. Maybe he's some crazed mountain man who hasn't had contact with another person in years. I mentally shrugged. *Eh, nobody's perfect. Besides, apart from Dax, this is the most attention a man has given me in...ever!*

"So, I take it that means you're single, then?" he asked hopefully.

"I am." Somehow his grin widened. I looked down at the phone in my hands and asked quietly, "Are you?"

"Yes," he replied quickly. I looked back up at him and gave him a shy smile. He said nothing as his eyes flitted excitedly over my face. Then he forcefully shook his head. "Sorry. I um, I'll leave you to your phone call." He started to stand, but I touched my hand to his arm. His whole body flinched and his head whipped to face me.

"You can stay...if you want." I *really* didn't want him to leave the room. I told myself it was because I was worried I'd get sick again or pass out or something, and needed someone to look out for me, but honestly, I just didn't want Phoenix to go. The thought of him leaving my side caused physical pain in my chest. I'd never experienced anything like this before; I'd had crushes, but this was something different.

"Are you sure?" At my slight nod, Phoenix sat back down on the bed and held out his hand. After *actually* almost passing out because I was just that smooth when it came to men, I slowly placed mine on top, linking our fingers together and marvelling at how much larger his warm, strong palm was than mine. He ran his thumb over the back of my knuckles and gave me a beautiful smile.

Before I did something stupid like kick off my underwear and offer my ass to him, I turned my attention back to the phone in my hand and dialed Dax's number.

"It's me," I answered when he picked up.

"Oh. My. Gawd," he replied dramatically. "*There* you are! I've been calling you all night!"

"Sorry," I started, but before I could offer more, Dax was on a roll.

"I was about to drive to the forest and look for you myself! Which meant I'd have to rent a Rascal to roll my fat ass up those hills, so you're lucky you *finally* called me or you'd owe me a rental fee. Now, tell me what was so damn important that you forgot to call. You better hope you either have broken limbs or are shacking up with a hot park ranger."

Phoenix's eyes were large, telling me he'd heard everything my loud, snarky friend just said. "Um...it's kind of both," I whispered into the mouthpiece. Whispering didn't do me any good; Phoenix scrubbed a hand over his mouth, unsuccessfully hiding a smile.

"Bullshit," Dax spat. "I'd know if you broke a bone because I'd *better* be your emergency contact. And my sweet, virginal Roar wouldn't shack up with anyone." I desperately punched at the volume button, trying to lower Dax's voice so Phoenix wouldn't hear it, but his eyes were wide again. *Thanks a lot, Dax.* "So, stop trying to make this dramatic and interesting and just tell me you forgot to call."

"I *didn't* forget to call," I argued. "I had an accident. I fell off of a small cliff and banged myself up. A few...park rangers?" I looked to Phoenix for confirmation, and he bounced his head back and forth again. *Close enough.* "Rangers found me and one brought me to his cabin to look after me."

"Are you serious?" Dax asked with concern in his voice. "Is that where you're calling from? I didn't recognize the number."

"Yeah, his name is Phoenix and he's been taking care of me all night."

"Holy shit," my friend breathed. "I'm sorry I snapped at you. Jesus, Roar; are you okay? What do you mean you banged yourself up?"

"I've just got a few bruised ribs and a concussion."

"Just? *Just?*" He sounded like he may explode. "You don't *just* have a concussion, Roar. That's serious. You're gonna be laid up for a few days. Do you need me to come get you? I have to work tonight, but you can stay here with Justin. I'm sure he'll look after you." My lip curled at the thought. Phoenix surprised me by holding his free hand out for the phone. Though I was confused, I handed it over.

"Hello, Dax. This is Phoenix. I've been looking after Rory and I'd feel better if he stays with me so that I can keep an eye on his progress. My friend lives next door and is a doctor-" he did that head bobble thing again, "So he'll be looked after. I don't think he should be moved right now and he needs his rest. I'm happy to help him with anything he needs." A slow smile crossed Phoenix's lips at whatever Dax was saying. "No, I'm not an axe murderer." I rolled my eyes, but stopped when colors burst behind them. "No, I'm not a sexual predator either." Phoenix barked a laugh. "No, not even if he asks nicely." I hid my red face behind my free hand. "I promise I'll take good care of your friend. Okay, yes, your *best* friend. And I promise to call you if he gets worse. Thanks, Dax. Okay, just a sec."

Phoenix handed the phone back to me. "Yes?" I asked into it nervously.

"Once your brain gets better, you better bone that." Once again, I pressed the volume button. "Wait, is he hot? Someone can sound hot over the phone but look like a bag of potatoes in person. *Please* tell me he's hot."

"He is," I barely whispered.

"Okay then, go for it. This is high quality porn material right here!" Dax turned on his movie announcer voice. "An injured virgin. A hot ranger. All alone in a cabin in the woods. Can he be healed with his dick? We'll find out in-"

"Okay, goodbye." I hung up the phone and handed it back to Phoenix, who was once again scrubbing a hand over his mouth. "Sorry about him. He's a little..." My bruised brain couldn't come up with a word better than "Weird."

Phoenix chuckled. "He seemed nice. And he obviously cares a lot about you, so he's okay in my book." He squeezed my hand which he was still holding and I smiled.

"Like I said, he's my family."

"What about other family? Is there anyone else you need to call?"

"I don't have anyone else," I shrugged. "When I turned eighteen, my parents kicked me out. They'd completed their duty and didn't want anything more to do with a gay son. That was four years ago and I've not heard a word from them. And I don't have any siblings, so it's just me and Dax. He had a hard time growing up too, and I guess we bonded over it. We've been best friends for over a decade."

Phoenix gave me a sad smile. "I'm so sorry about your parents, but I'm glad you had someone to look after you."

"Thanks. So what about your family? I mean...if that's not too personal." *Shit.* He had a legitimate reason to ask about mine, but I had no excuse besides curiosity about my sexy savior.

"Of course not. You can ask me anything, sweetheart." My heart fluttered at the endearment, but I tried not to read too much into it. Maybe he was one of those people who called everyone sweetheart or honey. "I lost my parents many years ago."

"I'm sorry," I offered, squeezing his hand.

"Thank you. They were good people; my father was fair but firm, and taught me what it meant to be a great man and leader. My mother was very kind; she never met a person she didn't like, and did so much to help our community." Phoenix's gorgeous green eyes shimmered as he remembered his folks, who he obviously adored.

"They sound wonderful."

He lifted my hand to kiss my knuckles and my breath caught in my chest. He whispered "Thank you" again before sighing. "I also have a brother, but we don't speak." I was curious as to why, but felt it wasn't my business to ask. I figured maybe it was a matter of them drifting apart after the trauma of losing their parents. It was sad, but it happened sometimes.

Phoenix shook his head. "Anyway, like I told Dax, I'd like for you to stay here so that I may keep watch over you. My friends Rowan and Stone are close by and will help in anyway they can. Is that okay with you, Rory? I want you here, but I would never force you. Do you feel comfortable staying with me?"

The hope in his eyes nearly killed me. Phoenix wanted me here; I could feel it. I knew I shouldn't be alone until I was fully healed, but *did* I feel comfortable enough to stay with him? He'd been nothing but kind and patient since I woke up, and he obviously took great care of me when I was asleep; he even carried me halfway across the park! Plus, he did live on state land, so his job here was probably through the government. That meant he would have been background checked and vetted to the extreme. But even if I didn't know any of that, the feeling I got when I was near him was enough to tell me I was safe by his side. He'd look after me and care for me; I knew it instinctively. Besides, the thought of leaving him made me sick to my stomach again. So did the thought of staying alone with Justin.

"If you're sure you don't mind, I'd like to stay here with you. You've taken such good care of me and I can't thank you enough for that."

Phoenix's smile lit up his face. "You don't need to thank me. It's my pleasure to take care of you. I'll do everything I can to make you comfortable and happy." He kissed my hand again and I had to remind myself to keep breathing. Then, a knock sounded on what I assumed was his front door. "That will be my friends. Are you sure you're okay with meeting them?"

I nodded. "Especially the one with pain killers." Phoenix chuckled as he tucked the blankets around me tighter, covering me all the way up to my chin.

"Come in," he said in a voice that wasn't much louder than the one he'd been using to speak to me. I didn't think there was any way his friends could hear him, but I was surprised by the sound of a door latch opening. *Maybe his front door is just on the other side of the wall.* I hadn't seen any of his house except for his bedroom.

Phoenix smiled over his shoulder at the door to his friends, whom I still couldn't see. "You may enter." His friends must have been waiting for permission to come into his room, which I found a little odd. Dax made himself at home when he came to my place. He'd even go in and raid my fridge when I wasn't at home.

Two men walked into Phoenix's bedroom and my eyes widened at the sight of them. They were both well over six feet tall. One of them looked to be built strong and fit like Phoenix. He had dark brown hair, a smooth face like me and pretty ice blue eyes. The other had a shaved head, a scruffy grayish black beard and light green eyes that were lovely, but nowhere near as captivating as Phoenix's. The man also looked like he was smuggling bowling balls under his t-shirt. I'd never seen someone so muscular.

All three men were sex personified. I wondered what in the hell was in the water around here and if I could buy it by the gallon. But as gorgeous as the other two men were (which was pretty freaking gorgeous), I had no interest in them. My eyes had wandered over their bodies for a moment, but were drawn back to Phoenix. He was truly the most handsome man I'd ever seen. Beyond that, when I looked at him, my soul settled.

"Sweetheart, I'd like to introduce you to my friends," Phoenix announced and my heart stammered again at the term. It was like he was laying claim to me in front of these other men. That, or I was blowing this way out of proportion. *I'll listen to what he calls them to see if the word is just for me.* "This is Rowan," he said, pointing to the clean shaven man, "And that's Stone." His finger pointed to the ball smuggler.

"Nice to meet you," I replied, looking between the two men. "Phoenix told me you two helped save my life. Thank you so much."

"Don't mention it," Stone replied with a shrug. It almost sounded like a threat coming from the beefy man.

"I'm just glad Phoenix found you when he did," Rowan replied. He stepped to Phoenix's side and held a hand out to me. "Rory, it's so nice to meet you. How are you feeling?"

I unburied my arm from beneath the covers to shake Rowan's hand. When I did, the corner of the blankets fell down, exposing one side of my chest. Phoenix was quick to cover it back up, making Stone snort a laugh. I didn't see what was so funny; I thought it was sweet that he was making sure I was warm.

"I feel like I fell off of a cliff," I replied, making Rowan smile. "My side's hurting a lot and my head is killing me."

"I brought something that I think will help." Rowan lifted his other hand, producing a bag which he placed on the bed. He stuck his hand in the top and pulled out a small ceramic pot. "This is an ointment I made for you to help with your pain. It contains capsaicin and peppermint oil." I immediately understood Phoenix's earlier head bobble; Rowan wasn't a doctor, he was some sort of holistic healer. I didn't care; at this point I'd take a shaman shaking a turtle shell at me if it helped.

Rowan turned to Phoenix and handed him the pot. "Rub it on his ribs and temples three times a day." Phoenix nodded and placed the jar on the nightstand. I won't lie; I got a thrill thinking about Phoenix rubbing his big hands over my body while tending to my injuries. Rowan turned his attention back to me. "It may tingle or even burn a bit," he said with a pained expression. "But it will help. The spices work on nerves that carry pain signals." I'd take a tingle over the misery I was feeling any day.

Rowan reached into his bag again and produced a thermos. "This is tea brewed with ginger and tumeric. It will help settle your stomach plus work as a pain reliever and anti-inflammatory." He handed the thermos to Phoenix, who then gave the mug to me.

"Thank you for all of this," I told him seriously as I wrapped my fingers around the warm cup. "I really appreciate it. And I never knew herbs could be used like this." I'd heard ginger ale could settle stomachs, but that was the extent of my knowledge. I took a long drink of the tea, which warmed me from the inside out. The slightly spicy flavor tingled on my tongue. "This is delicious." Definitely better than any medicine I'd tasted. "Thank you."

Rowan's lips stretched into a wide grin. "It's no trouble. I love being able to help out when I can." I could already tell

Rowan was a sweet soul from his earnest words and kind eyes.

"Thank you for everything," Phoenix told his friend, patting his back. "Would you mind examining his injuries now?"

"Not at all."

I took my cue and pushed the blankets off of my chest, letting them pool around my hips. Rowan and Stone quickly turned their backs to me and I looked to Phoenix in confusion.

"It's okay," he told Rowan with a touch to his shoulder. His friend slowly turned around to face me again.

"I'll wait in the living room," Stone announced before stepping out of the bedroom, closing the door behind him.

"I'm sorry; I didn't mean to make him uncomfortable," I said quickly. "I figured it wouldn't matter since we were all men." I looked to Rowan. "I'm wearing underwear."

He gave me an adoring smile and Phoenix stepped to my side, taking my hand. "No sweetheart, you didn't do anything wrong. Stone just left out of respect."

"It's okay; he can come back in if he wants," I offered.

Phoenix looked torn, and I wondered if it wasn't just *me* Stone was respecting. Rowan spoke up. "This will only take a minute." Phoenix took my thermos and a step away from the bed to allow Rowan to slide in closer to me, but he didn't drop my hand from his large palm.

"May I sit?" Rowan asked, pointing to the bed beside me.

"Of course," I answered, scooting my legs over to make room. It wasn't until he also got a nod from Phoenix that he sat.

"Okay, I'm going to feel your ribs now." He placed a big hand on either side of my chest, gently pressing his fingers into my skin and lowering them down my flanks. I hissed at the pain that spread over my right side. "Sorry." Rowan gave me a tight smile and continued to feel. "Okay, I still don't believe anything is broken, but I'm feeling some swelling under your skin. You'll probably get colorful over the next few days as the bruises raise to the surface. I'd suggest soaking in a warm tub with Epsom salt to help with the bruising." He looked to Phoenix. "I think I've got some at home; if so, I'll bring it over."

Phoenix nodded and Rowan turned his head back to me. "Can you take a deep breath?" I tried, and winced at the pain it caused. "It's possible you've bruised your lung, too. Try to work on taking slow deep breaths to keep your lungs open. We don't want you getting pneumonia." Phoenix squeezed my hand and I looked to him, finding his face painted with worry.

"I know you're in a lot of pain," Rowan continued, "But I'm positive nothing's broken. Still, it will be awhile before you're feeling yourself again. Bruised ribs can take a couple of weeks or longer to heal. What do you do for a living?"

"I stock items at a grocery store." I blushed as I answered; Phoenix and his friends had impressive jobs with the state government. I put cereal on a shelf.

"You'll need to take time off. You can't be lifting and stretching while you're trying to heal."

"I can't afford to take that much time off of work," I replied, blushing even harder. "I don't get paid for sick leave and if I don't have a paycheck for three weeks, I won't be able to afford my rent." I worked for a small mom and pop store. I had crappy insurance and didn't accrue sick leave or vacation time.

Phoenix squeezed my hand again and bent down to place a gentle kiss on my knuckles. "Sweetheart, all you need to be worried about is getting better. I'll take care of the rest." I didn't know what that meant exactly, but I believed him. The sincerity of his voice and the gentleness of his touch told me I could trust him to give me anything I needed. My cheeks cooled and my worry faded. I was confident Phoenix would take care of everything.

"Thank you," I whispered, and he gave me a dazzling smile in return.

"Okay, let's take a look at your head," Rowan continued. He placed his hands around my skull and carefully squeezed. "You still have a knot here, but that will shrink over the next few days. I know you have a headache, but have you had any other symptoms like blurry vision or dark spots or colors behind your eyes?"

"If I roll my eyes, I get colors, but nothing's blurry."

"Good," he smiled. "Has there been any leakage from your ears or nose?"

"Not that I know of." I looked to Phoenix, who shook his head no at his friend.

"Excellent. And your speech sounds clear and not slurred, so those are all great signs." He held my eyelids open and pulled out his cell phone. He shone the beam from its flashlight into my eyes quickly. "Your pupils are reactive, so that's great too. I think you're on the mend." He smiled and patted my shoulder. "You may get headaches from time to time as your brain continues to heal. Just be on the lookout for anything strange like memory changes, personality changes and trouble speaking.

Other than that, you just need rest and relaxation and you'll be good as new. You may walk around when you feel like it, but don't do any strenuous exercise."

"You're wicked smart with this stuff," I offered, and Rowan gave me a wide smile.

"Thank you, Rory. I'm just happy to help." He squeezed my shoulder and stood up, facing Phoenix. "Make sure he gets lots of fluids. He may not have much of an appetite for a few days, but he still needs to eat what he can. Fresh fruits and vegetables are best and will help his brain tissue heal more quickly."

"Thank you." Rowan bowed his head to Phoenix, who turned to me. "Do you have any food allergies?"

"Pineapples give me hives."

"Bastard fruits," Phoenix grumped. "I never liked them." I snorted a laugh and immediately paid for it with a pain in my forehead. I cradled my face in my hand and Phoenix once again squeezed my palm. "I think I need to put your ointment on now. I want you to have some relief." I was capable of rubbing the cream on myself, but I wasn't about to stop him.

"I'll wait with Stone," Rowan offered. "It was so nice to meet you, Rory. I hope you feel better soon. I'm sure I'll see you later." He smiled and left the bedroom, shutting Phoenix and me inside alone.

Phoenix took the jar from the nightstand, but I cleared my throat to stop him from dipping his fingers into the cream. "Could I please use the restroom before we start?" My bladder felt as if it were about to pop.

"Of course," he replied, nodding quickly. He placed the pot back on the nightstand. "I'm sorry; I didn't even think about that. The bathroom is right through there." He pointed to a doorway on the opposite side of the bed. Phoenix folded the blankets to the side, exposing my entire body to the cool air of the room. The extreme temperature difference made me shiver. "I'll get you some warm clothes." I chewed on my lip; I didn't think I could wait to use the toilet that long. "When you're finished," he added, and I blew out a sigh of relief.

Phoenix took my hands and slowly pulled me into an upright position. He pivoted my hips so that my legs were hanging over the side of the bed and supported me by the armpits as I stood. "You got it?" I nodded slightly and took a step forward. *Not too bad.* After two more steps, however, my head swam and my legs trembled. "It's okay, I've got you." Phoenix scooped me into his arms, keeping my injured side away from his body. "Is this okay?"

"Perfect," I whispered. We stared into each other's eyes as he carried me across the room. He was sure of his movements, not even needing to look away to see where he was going. His strong body was firm and warm against mine, but he cradled me so gently in his arms like I was something precious.

"Here we go." I hadn't even noticed we'd entered a different room. Phoenix looked away from me to turn on the light to the bathroom, breaking the trance between us. He stepped until we were in front of the toilet and set me on my feet. "I'll be right outside if you need me." He left the room and closed the solid wood door behind him.

I shimmied down my underwear as my legs started to shake. Even though they hadn't been injured when I fell, my entire body was weak. I didn't think my legs would support me, so I sat down to piss. It seemed to go on forever, giving me a chance to look around. The bathroom was a good size. The walls were made of the same pretty honey-stained wood logs as Phoenix's bedroom. He had a hunter green shower curtain and bath mat on the floor. The toilet and pedestal sink were bright white.

I finished, flushed and stood up way too quickly. My body teetered and I reached out to grab the basin of the sink to steady myself. "Phoenix?" The door opened quickly and in a blink, Phoenix was before me. "I got dizzy."

"It's okay, sweetheart. I'm right here." He sank to one knee in front of me and I wondered what in the hell was happening until he grabbed my underwear off the ground and pulled them up my legs. He straightened the waistband around my hips and stood up again.

"Oh my god, I'm so sorry." My cheeks heated with embarrassment. "I forgot they were down."

"Hey, it's okay," he soothed, cupping my cheeks in his hands. He seemed totally at peace with just having seen my dick and I didn't know what to think about that. *Was he not impressed?* Granted I was soft; hell, even when I was hard, my length was proportionate to my body size and not the biggest thing in the world, but...he just saw my dick! *How is he so chill about this?*

He steadied me in front of the sink so that I could wash my hands and then scooped me into his arms again. This time as he carried me to the bed, he didn't look into my eyes. *I made it weird. What if he thinks I purposely flashed him my junk? He obviously didn't like it. God, of course he didn't like it! Look at him! He's huge and hot and probably has a baseball bat in his boxers!*

Phoenix placed me on his bed again, resting me against the pillows piled on the headboard. "I'll get you those clothes now," he said without so much as a glance to my face. He turned and walked to his dresser, and my heart sank. Something changed between us and it was all my fault. He'd been so nice to me and I made him uncomfortable.

"I'm really sorry," I whispered, and Phoenix glanced over his shoulder at me. A look of confusion marred his handsome face. "I didn't mean to make things awkward. I really did forget my underwear were down. I just got dizzy and scared and called for you. I'd never do that on purpose. I hope you can forgive me."

"Oh, Rory, no." He took three giant steps and was at my side. He sat on the edge of the bed and took both of my hands. "Sweetheart, you didn't do anything wrong. I was worried I made *you* uncomfortable." I narrowed my eyes in confusion and Phoenix sighed. "I'm trying to be a gentleman because of your condition, but I can't help the way my body reacts to you."

What is he talking about? My eyes trailed over his body, looking for clues. I found a big one pressing against the front of his boxers. "Oh shit!" *Smooth, Roar.*

"I'm sorry," Phoenix replied quickly. "I promise you're safe with me. I would never take advantage of you. I don't want to scare you. I-"

"I'm not scared," I interrupted. "I'm beyond confused about how I could affect you like that, but I'm definitely not scared."

He looked offended over my lack of self-esteem. "Rory, you are the most beautiful creature I've ever laid eyes on. Your body is exquisite; I can't help *but* be affected by you."

"Thank you." *Was that a weird thing to say? Hey, thanks for getting a boner? My god, I'm so bad at this.* Phoenix smiled at me, calming my inner struggle. "I think you're gorgeous," I blurted out, my cheeks heating again. *Hell, I'm already this far in; might as well go for it.* "Your body is incredible and your face is like, ridiculously handsome and even the way you treat me is attractive. You're just the total package." *I hope all this extra blood flushing my face doesn't pop my bruised brain.*

Phoenix's grin stretched across his whole face as he stroked my heated flesh with the backs of his fingers. "Thank you, sweetheart. You don't know what that means to me." He leaned in and I held my breath as his lips gently touched my cheek. The bristly scruff of his beard tickled my skin and his earthy, woody scent filled my nostrils. It was the most incredible thing I'd ever experienced. I didn't even care it took a jumbled brain to get it.

Phoenix was still smiling brightly when he pulled away from me. He ran his fingers through my hair, and I flinched when they brushed against the lump on my scalp. "Oh shit, I'm so sorry; I'm supposed to be taking care of you, not fondling you."

"I like the fondling," I argued before I could stop myself, making Phoenix laugh.

"Me too, but still..." he grabbed the small jar from the nightstand. "I better get this on you or Rowan will have my hide."

"Okay." I agreed easily because one, pain relief sounded *great*, and two, Phoenix rubbing ointment on my body was still technically fondling.

He dipped his fingers into the jar, scooping out a large white blob of lotion. "Tell me if I'm too rough, okay? I don't want to hurt you."

I couldn't answer because I was momentarily stunned at how dirty and wonderful his words sounded. "Oh, right, yeah, I'll tell you," I mumbled after staring at him for way too long. Phoenix didn't even try to hide his smile as he touched his fingers to my side.

He gently massaged the ointment onto my skin in large, smooth circles. The herbs tingled on my skin, leaving a slight burning sensation in their wake. "Rowan was right; that does burn a little," I told Phoenix as he finished applying the lotion to my ribs.

"I feel it on my fingers," he agreed. "Is it too much? I can wipe it off of you and ask him to make some that's a little weaker."

"No it's okay. That just means it's doing its job, right?"

Phoenix smiled. "Let's hope so. Is it okay if I put it on your temples?" I nodded and he got another pile on his fingers. He massaged it gently onto each side of my face.

"Mm, I love the peppermint smell," I said, taking a deep whiff as he closed the jar and put it back on the nightstand. "It reminds me of Christmas."

"I take it you love Christmas?" Phoenix asked, taking my hand in his. He seemed to want to touch me as much as possible and I sure as hell wasn't going to stop him.

"*Everybody* loves Christmas," I shrugged and he chuckled. "But yeah, it's my favorite time of year. Dax and I always binge on Hallmark movies and eat sugar cookies until we're sick."

"It sounds like you two have a lot of fun together." His eyes were sparkling and he still had a smile on his face. He didn't seem jealous; more like he was interested in hearing about my life.

"We do. We used to spend a lot more time together before *Justin* entered the picture."

"Who's Justin?" he asked curiously, cocking his head.

"Dax's boyfriend," I snarled.

"Okay, I take it you don't like Justin," he chuckled.

"He's an ass. He treats Dax like crap, but anytime I try to talk to Dax about it, we fight, so I just keep my mouth shut. I just wish he could see how great he is and find someone who treats him the way he deserves to be treated."

"You care a lot about him."

"Just as a friend," I reminded him, and Phoenix chuckled again.

"I know, sweetheart. It sounds like you are close to Dax the way I'm close to Rowan and Stone. They're my best friends and my family, but there could never be anything romantic between us."

"Exactly," I agreed, glad he understood. "I really like your friends, by the way. Rowan seems very sweet, and Stone...well, Stone didn't say much, but he helped save me, and that tells me everything I need to know about him."

"That means the world to me," he replied, squeezing my hand. "I'm sure you three will become great friends over time." Butterflies erupted in my gut; Phoenix was envisioning me being around for a while.

"Phoenix?" He raised his eyebrows, showing he was listening. "When I'm healed up and can go home...do you think you'll still want to see me? I mean, maybe you'd want to hang out? With just you and me? Not that

I wouldn't want to hang out with Rowan and Stone too. It's just...I don't know...Nevermind." *I. Suck. At. This.*

Phoenix didn't laugh at me, though. He dropped my hand and cupped both of my cheeks in his palms. "Rory, I think now that I've met you, I won't be able to live without you." *Oh my.* A shiver rocked through my body at his words. "Shit, I forgot your warm clothes. I'm a terrible caregiver."

"You're a wonderful caregiver," I argued. "And that shudder wasn't from being cold." Phoenix smiled and pressed another gentle kiss to my cheek. My eyes slid closed and I hummed gently. Too soon, he was gone. I peeled my eyelids open to see him digging through his dresser drawers. He stepped into a pair of dark jeans and pulled on a dark green Henley top. He grabbed some more clothes out of a different drawer and turned to face me.

The fabric of his shirt clung to his torso. His defined abs showed through, and the top corner of his tattoo peeked out of the open buttons. The dark denim of his jeans hugged his strong thighs and made my mouth water. *Good lord, how does someone put on* more *clothes and get sexier?*

"Here we go," he said as he returned to my side. "I've got some clothes for you to wear; your jeans won't be comfortable to relax in. Besides, I'd like to wash your outfit to get it fresh for you."

"You don't have to do that. You've done so much for me already."

"It's my pleasure." I took that as his polite way of saying he was going to do it whether I wanted him to or not.

"Thanks." He smiled and helped me into a black sweatshirt, which was at least two sizes too large. Then he lowered the blankets and shimmied a pair of gray sweatpants up my legs. They gaped off of my stomach, but it was okay since I was lying down. Phoenix rolled the bottoms of the legs up several inches so that my feet poked out the holes.

"Comfy?"

"Very," I smiled, loving the feel of his clothing on my body.

"And you look adorable." I blushed; nobody had ever called me adorable before. I'd heard 'nerd', 'shrimp', and 'fairy' a million times, but never adorable. "I know you're probably tired, but can you drink some more of the tea Rowan brought for you?" I'd forgotten about the tea with all the fondling. I nodded and Phoenix handed me the thermos. I tipped the liquid to my lips and drank. It was still warm and felt good in my stomach. I drained the mug and handed it back to Phoenix, who smiled. "Thank you." I tried to answer him, but a huge yawn took over my lips.

"Sorry."

"Don't be. You need your rest." He eased my glasses off of my nose and folded them up on the nightstand. "I'm going to talk with Rowan and Stone, but I'll just be in the next room if you need me."

I'd also forgotten his friends were here because, well, fondling. I started to thank Phoenix for the hundredth time, but had a better idea. I crooked my finger and he bent over, lowering his face to mine. I pressed a kiss to his scruffy jaw and heard a subtle gasp escape his lips.

"Thank you," he whispered. He tucked the blankets around my body and stroked my cheek again. "Rest well, sweetheart." He turned out the light as he left the room, and I was out almost as quickly.

Chapter Five

Phoenix

"Well, well, if it isn't Mr. Total Package himself," Stone teased as I joined him and Rowan in my living room. It wasn't that they'd been eavesdropping; as shifters, they couldn't help but overhear what was said in the next room.

"Jealous?" I asked with a shrug.

"Not a chance. My package puts your package to shame." He was joking, but it was also true. We were nude often from shifting and I'd seen Stone's package; I wasn't small by any means, but the man was a beast.

"Too bad for you Rory is only interested in *my* package," I shrugged again.

"Mm-hm. I heard about all the fondling going on in there."

"Oh calm down, I touched his cheek."

"His ass cheek?" he asked excitedly, but I just rolled my eyes.

"Well don't take this the wrong way," Rowan butted in, "But I hate you." I blinked in surprise at my friend. "Your mate is sweet and beautiful and right in the next room," he pouted, crossing his arms. I fought the urge to growl at him; he didn't want *my* mate, he wanted his own. "So I hate you."

"Just don't take it the wrong way," Stone added with a smirk.

"Of course not." I flopped down on the brown leather sofa next to Rowan. Stone was seated in my favorite spot, the matching recliner. It was extra wide and had massage and heat built in. He knew it was my favorite, and insisted on sitting there every time he visited. So, when I visited *his* place, I made sure to sit in his recliner and smoosh my butt around, messing with what he claimed were his "ass grooves" that took him years to create. We picked on and pestered each other, but the two men had my back on all of the important things. Speaking of which...

"I have a job for both of you." Rowan and Stone sat up straighter, listening for their instructions. "The guardrail needs replaced on the Deer Hill path where we found Rory. Until it's done, we need to mark off the trail so that no one else gets hurt. While it's closed, I'd like for you two to search the grounds at the bottom of the cliff. I want to make sure none of my mate's belongings were left behind."

The two of them looked at each other before looking back at me. "It's already done," Rowan offered. "After we prepared your cabin for Rory's arrival, we took some wood planks up to Deer Hill and replaced the railing. We wanted to make sure visitors were safe without delaying the trail opening today."

"Thank you," I smiled. "I know I can always count on you two." I wasn't surprised they anticipated the needs of the public; they were both smart, motivated men whom I was happy to have on my side.

"We also searched the area," Stone added. "The only thing we found was that." He pointed to my small kitchen table in the next room, where a few lumps of black plastic rested.

"What is it?" I asked as I rose from the couch and walked to the table.

"It *used* to be a camera," Stone answered.

I remembered something Rory said when I found him while in wolf form. *If I had my camera, I'd take your picture.* "Shit, it's his," I sighed. I picked up the remains and was able to make out a name brand. "Could I ask one of you for a favor?" I didn't hand out official jobs unless they were pack business. Requesting personal errands as tasks was no way to lead.

"Absolutely," Rowan answered. When I turned to look at them, Stone was nodding his head in agreement. They'd do anything to help me out, as I would do for them.

"Could one of you collect some things from town that I need for Rory? I would go, but I want to stay close to my mate in case he needs me. I'd like to buy him another one of these," I shook the plastic chunk in my hand, "Along with some fresh fruits and vegetables, and some comfortable clothes in size small." I'd seen the size on my mate's shirt when I took it off of him earlier. I loved seeing *my* clothing on Rory, but I also didn't want him tripping over them when he was able to get up and walk around more.

"I'd be happy to," Rowan smiled.

"Thank you." I retrieved my wallet from a bowl by the front door and gave him my bank card along with the chunk of camera that showed the model name. "Get anything else you think he might need as well."

"I think he might need a motorcycle," Stone replied, making his eyebrows dance.

"Then I guess it's a good thing Rowan is going shopping."

Stone shrugged. "It was worth a shot."

"I'll be back soon," Rowan promised, ignoring Stone. "And I'll make some more tea when I return."

"Thank you." Rowan nodded his head and disappeared out the door. Through the window, I saw him climb into the extended cab truck that we all shared. We mainly kept to ourselves and our land, with intermittent trips to town, so one vehicle to share was really all we needed.

"I'll be going too," Stone announced as he stood. "Don't worry about anything; just take care of your mate and I'll keep an eye open for any other trouble."

"Thanks, Stone." He rose from the recliner and shook my hand in a tight grip.

"You got it. And in case I haven't said it, I really *am* happy for you, Alpha." I gave him a smile and nod in thanks, and he too left my home.

*****

It'd been five hours since Rory fell back asleep. Rowan delivered the items he bought in town, and I had a meal prepared for my mate in the fridge. I sat in my recliner, waiting and listening for the first sign of Rory waking.

I jumped from my chair when I heard Rory's breathing change and his weight shifting against the mattress. I grabbed a tray of food from the refrigerator and tucked another full thermos of Rowan's tea under my arm.

I stepped into my bedroom and smiled at the sight of Rory rubbing his eyes with one hand and feeling the nightstand for his glasses with the other.

"Hey, sweetheart," I said quietly so I wouldn't startle him. "How are you feeling?"

"Sore, but a little better," he replied as he settled his glasses on his face and sat up against the headboard.

"I'm happy to hear it." If Rory and I were mated, he would have inherited my increased healing speed and would be feeling great by now. But, I didn't think he was *quite* ready for me to spill my seed inside him and bite my claiming mark into his neck. Humans could be tricky about such things. "Is it okay if I turn the light on?"

"Sure." Rory shielded his eyes as I illuminated the room. He blinked hard as his eyes acclimated to the light. "What's all that?" he asked as he looked at the tray in my hands.

"I brought you something to eat. Are you hungry?"

"Starving," he smiled.

A pang of guilt shot through my gut. "Rory, I'm sorry. I should have woken you to bring you food. My god, you probably haven't eaten in twenty four hours. I was trying to let you get the rest you needed, but-"

"Hey, it's okay," he interrupted, raising a hand to stop my babbling. "I *did* need rest. Food was the last thing on my mind, especially when I was feeling sick. I don't think I could have eaten before now anyway."

My mate was infallibly sweet; he had to feel like shit, but he was trying to comfort me. "Well, I'm glad you're feeling up to eating now." I sat beside him on the bed and held out the tray, which held strawberries, orange and apple slices, broccoli stalks, carrot sticks and ranch dip. "Is this okay? I'd be happy to make you something else."

"It looks amazing." His stomach agreed as it let out a long growl. "Thank you."

"You're welcome." I placed the dish on his knees and gave him a wide smile as he took the mug from my hand. "I was thinking maybe you'd want to take a bath after you eat. I had Rowan pick up some of the salt he suggested and some bath oil. Also, I bought you some clothes in your size which you may be more comfortable in."

Rory blinked hard. "You did all of that for *me*?"

"Of course. I promised to take care of you." He stared at me for a moment before wincing and rubbing his chest. "What's wrong?"

He shook his head and looked away. "Nothing." He rubbed his chest again. *Something* was bothering him and I wanted to do anything I could to make it better.

"Sweetheart, you can tell me. What is it?"

A pretty blush took over his cheeks. "It's just that everything you're doing for me is so wonderful. I...I wanted to kiss you, but I was worried you wouldn't want me to. When I didn't, my chest started hurting."

Sweet Rory was feeling the effects of the mate pull. Our bodies were calling out to one another. If he didn't answer the call, it would cause him physical pain or illness.

"You *never* have to worry that I don't want to kiss you."

Rory's eyes widened as they landed on me. "Really?"

I gently brushed a stray lock of hair away from his forehead. "Really." His gaze flicked between my eyes and his breath quickened. His tongue trailed along his bottom lip, making his pink skin glisten. Rory slowly leaned in toward me and I copied his actions as his pretty brown eyes slid closed.

My pulse raced as our lips touched. His flesh was soft and moist against mine. I gently sucked his plump bottom lip between my own and Rory whimpered the most beautiful sound. I pecked his lips tenderly and lovingly until he pulled back, his eyes still closed and his mouth slightly open.

"Wow," he whispered. His eyes slowly opened and he swallowed thickly. "Was...was that okay?"

"It was perfect." I cupped his cheek in my hand and caressed his smooth cheek with my thumb. "Was it okay for you?"

"It was incredible," he replied quickly. "I was just checking to see if I did it right." A blush returned to his cheeks. "I've never kissed anyone before."

My heart nearly burst from my chest. Being the first and only man he ever kissed was a gift I'd treasure for eternity. "Really?"

Rory gave a slight nod. "Like I told you, I grew up in a very conservative town, and being gay was looked down upon. Ever since I moved to the city, I've been busy with work and spending all of my free time I can with Dax, so I never met anyone I liked." He swallowed thickly. "I...I really like *you*, Phoenix. I know we haven't known each other long, and it's okay if you don't feel the same way, but-"

"Rory," I interrupted, caressing his heated cheek again, "I really like you too." I felt so much more for him than that; I loved him now and always, but my poor mate seemed overwhelmed and I didn't want to put too much on him. "You're sweet and beautiful and funny; I hate *how* we met, but I'll be forever grateful that we did. I want to be with you, if that's what you want too."

Rory's eyes nearly bugged out of his head. "*Be* with me? Like...as a boyfriend? Or...as a lover?" He whispered the last question like it was a dirty secret. Blood pooled in my groin and my dick thickened at the suggestion.

"Both," I whispered back, and Rory gasped. "But like I said, only if it's what you want too." I'd never force my mate into anything, but his rejection would send me spiraling into a life of pain and depression. Again, probably too much to tell him right now.

"It is," he answered, and my heart fluttered. "I don't know if I'll be very good at it, but the thought of *not* being with you gives me that pain in my chest again. That's got to be a sign, right?"

"Definitely a sign," I smiled. "And don't worry about if you will be good at it or not; your body knows what to do. When we're making love, just let go and allow your instincts to take over. Besides that, it we be impossible for me not to enjoy being with you. I care for you so deeply and find your body so delectable, our lovemaking will be a wondrous, earth-moving experience, I'm sure."

A quiet whimper left Rory's lips and he shifted his legs against the mattress. "Oh, I, um..." his cheeks burned red and he cleared his throat. "I meant I didn't know if I'd be very good at being a boyfriend. I'll try to be the very best boyfriend I can to you, but I don't have any experience. I may make mistakes, but I promise to learn from them and do everything I can to make you happy." His gaze trailed away from me as he added, "That's good to know about the...*other* stuff too. I won't lie; I'm still a little nervous for when the time comes, but what you said does make me feel better."

Oops. I'd been so focused on wanting to get my hands on Rory's perfect body, I'd misunderstood his concerns. "I know you'll be the best boyfriend," I told him with a smile, and got a shy grin in return. "And when the time comes for more, you don't have to be nervous. I promise I'll take good care of you." His cheeks stained pink once more as he nodded. "But for now, I just want you to focus on eating."

"Oh, right; I almost forgot." Rory turned his attention to the food I brought for him. He drained the tea from his mug and placed it on the nightstand before attacking the fruits and vegetables. He made short work of the broccoli and carrots. I was pleased he had such a good appetite; his body was on the mend.

My pleasure turned to pain when Rory ate the fruit on his tray. He made sweet little hums and moans that had my dick as hard as a rock in my jeans. I couldn't turn my eyes from the way the tip of his tongue peeked out between his lips to collect the juice that dripped down his chin as he bit into the luscious berries. He wasn't trying to tease me; he was just enjoying his lunch, but I was about five seconds from passing out or jizzing my pants and honestly, I was okay with either one since both options would give me relief.

"I'm sorry, I'm being rude," Rory offered after sucking his finger clean of orange juice and nearly killing me. "Would you like some?" He picked up a plump strawberry by the leaves and offered me the red berry. I wasn't hungry, but I sure as hell wasn't turning down this opportunity.

I wrapped my lips around the fruit and bit down into the juicy flesh. A trail of sweet juice trickled down my chin and Rory was quick to wipe it away with his thumb. I released the strawberry from my mouth and took my mate's thumb between my lips, gently sucking it clean. Rory's gaze darkened and his mouth parted as he stared at my mouth.

I swallowed the berry and sucked on his thumb harder until his entire digit was in my mouth. I swirled my tongue around his flesh, tasting the sweetness that clung to it. Rory whimpered as I bobbed my head back and forth, sucking his thumb the way I longed to suck his cock. I slowly pulled back until his wet thumb popped free from my lips. We were both panting and gazing into one another's eyes.

"I really want to kiss you again," Rory admitted before trailing his tongue along his bottom lip. It was too much. I crashed my mouth to his. This was not the gentle, tender kiss from before. This was giving into my - *our* desires to taste. I pressed my tongue to the seam of his plump, delicious lips and Rory opened readily for me.

My tongue slid against his and I sighed at my first taste of my mate's sweet flavor. I licked every inch of his mouth, sampling each surface of his cheeks. I ran my tongue over every ridge on the roof of Rory's mouth, making him shudder against me.

My sweet Rory was timid when it came to his turn to taste. He slowly pressed his tongue into my mouth and licked against my own slick appendage, feeling each bump of my taste buds. He gently studied the surface of the roof of my mouth and drew circular designs on the flesh of my cheeks. I sucked each of his sweet breaths into my own lungs as he steadily and methodically took his fill of my flavor.

When his tongue retreated from my mouth, my restraint snapped. I cupped both of his smooth cheeks in my big hands and shoved my own tongue between his lips. I desperately licked against him as Rory moaned wantonly, throwing fuel on my fire. I gingerly guided his head back toward his pillow.

He ripped his lips from mine and I was worried I'd gone too far. "Oops, I'm so sorry," Rory said, looking down at the blankets. I followed his gaze to find the tray tipped over and a few orange peels spread over the covers.

"My fault, sweetheart." I was the one who shifted his position and knocked the tray over. Besides that, I didn't give two shits about the blankets right now. I piled the fruit on the plate and reached across Rory's beautiful body to place it on the nightstand. Then I gripped the blankets in my fist and shoved them off of the bed. I couldn't stand them being between us any longer.

"Shit, that's hot," Rory breathed. His eyes widened and his cheeks pinked, making me believe he hadn't meant to say it out loud. I gave him a wicked smile and eased him the rest of the way back until his head was cradled against his pillow and his body was flat against the mattress. I lay on my side, nuzzled against him.

"You know what I think is hot?" Rory gave a little shake of his head. I placed my palm on his stomach and stroked him in smooth, gentle circles. "The sight of your beautiful little body in my clothes." I leaned over him and pecked his lips. "Having you here in my bed with me." I trailed my lips to his ear and nibbled lightly on its lobe. "Everything about you."

"Phoenix, please." I pulled back to stare into his eyes, which were wide and desperate. His breathing was ragged and his bottom lip was trapped between his teeth.

"What do you need, Rory?" I wanted to give him everything he desired. "Anything, sweetheart; just tell me."

"I don't know," he whispered, and his cheeks flushed. "I just know I need you. My pulse is racing and my body feels like it's burning from the inside. I need your touch."

My dick throbbed in my jeans. "Oh, Rory, I feel the same way." I leaned in and took his lips with mine, kissing him fiercely and deeply. "Can I touch you?" I asked when I released him. I wanted to double check and get his permission; this was all new to him and I'd never want to push too far.

"Please." At Rory's plea, I trailed my fingers to the hem of my sweatshirt he was wearing and slipped them under the fabric. I caressed the smooth skin of his stomach and eased the shirt up his chest until it was tucked under his chin.

"Look at you," I whispered, rubbing my hand over his trunk, careful not to touch where his ribs were injured. "Your body is beautiful, sweetheart."

"You don't think I'm too skinny?"

"I think you're absolutely perfect."
Rory's lips curled up into a pretty smile and I
couldn't help but to kiss them. "Is it okay if I
take this off?" I asked, tugging on the hem
of the sweatshirt. Rory nodded and I eased
his arms out of the sleeves before lifting the
shirt free of his head. I tossed the fabric to
the floor and went back to gently caressing
his stomach and chest.

"Can I take yours off too?" Rory asked
quietly. My blood burned and I couldn't nod
fast enough. My mate reached out to remove
my shirt and flinched when he stretched his
right arm.

"Here, I'll get it," I offered. I didn't
want him hurting himself worse. I gripped
the bottom of my Henley top in my hand and
pulled it from my body in one smooth
movement.

Rory swallowed thickly as his eyes
roved over my chest. "I love your body,

Phoenix." He touched his fingers to my abdomen and felt along the dips and ridges of my muscles. "You're so strong and sexy." His hand thoroughly explored my stomach and chest before sliding up my neck and cupping my cheek. "I love your beard. And you have the most gorgeous eyes I've ever seen." He shook his head. "I can't believe I'm with someone so handsome."

I puffed up with pride and pecked his lips. "I feel the same way." Rory's jaw dropped and I took the opportunity to attack his lips again. I sank my tongue into his mouth and swallowed up his sweet whimpers.

I kissed a line across his jaw and down his neck. Rory moaned as I sucked a pretty purple bruise onto his throat. "That feels so good," he panted as he clutched my side. I placed my hand on his chest and caressed down the smooth skin of his stomach until my fingers bumped against the waistband of his pants.

"Rory, can I take-"

"Yes," he interrupted before I could finish my question. I slipped my hand under the fabric easily, as it gaped from his slim body. I pushed the pants down, the wispy hairs on his legs tickling my fingers as I went. I'd seen him in only his briefs before, but hadn't let myself fully enjoy the breathtaking sight. Now I soaked up every detail as my gaze studied his body.

My breath caught when my eyes landed on the thick lump in his underwear. I could make out the slim length of his dick as it pressed against the fabric, along with the circular wet spot over his cut tip. Rory squirmed under my gaze and I didn't want him to feel as if he was being examined or on display. I popped the button of my jeans and lowered their zipper. When I raised my eyes to Rory's, I found they were wide and hungry. I shimmied the denim down my legs and my mate gasped at the sight of my hard cock tenting the fabric of my boxers.

Rory's fists pumped open and closed and his tongue wet his lips as he stared at my bulge. "You can touch, sweetheart," I whispered before placing a gentle kiss to his cheek. "It's yours."

He didn't look up as his hand slowly inched toward me. His fingers spread and gently brushed along my length. I hummed when I felt the subtle tingle that came from contact with my mate even through my boxers. Rory pet my dick in unsure movements like he was greeting an unfamiliar dog. I smiled at the thought; in a way, he actually was.

"Don't be shy," I told him, once again peppering his face with kisses. "Everything you do feels so good." Rory gulped and wrapped his fingers around my base. He stroked along my length and I hissed at the feel of the soft cotton rubbing against my heated flesh. "Just like that, sweetheart." He gripped harder and moved his wrist faster, seemingly more confident in his actions. His touch felt amazing, but I wasn't satisfied. I needed to feel him. "Can I touch you too?"

Rory's hand stopped and his eyes snapped to mine. "Okay."

"Sweetheart, if we're moving too fast, let's stop."

"I don't want to stop," he countered, once again rubbing his chest. "It's just...Well, I haven't seen you, but I've felt you." He gave my dick a gentle squeeze and I couldn't help but moan. "And I've felt myself..." Rory blushed and I grinned at my naughty mate. "And we're definitely not the same. I just don't want you to be disappointed."

"Oh, sweet Rory, I could never be disappointed when it comes to you. If that's your only concern, push it away. You're absolutely perfect in my eyes." I sealed my promise with a tender kiss to his lips.

He blew out a long breath. "Okay." Rory nodded determinedly. "Please touch me, baby." He flinched and his brows folded in with worry. "Is that okay?"

"So much better than okay." I attacked his mouth again, overwhelmed by the sound of the endearment on my mate's lips. This time, Rory gave as good as he got, boldly licking against my tongue and moaning as our flavors mixed. I slid my hand along his stomach until I cupped his hard dick in my palm. I stroked him through the thin material of his briefs and felt warmth on my fingers as pre-cum leaked from him.

My wolf clawed and paced inside me, desperate to claim and own. Rory wasn't ready for that yet, and I wouldn't take him until I'd explained everything to him. But I needed more than this. I craved more than touching my mate through a barrier, no matter how thin.

I tucked my fingers in the waistband of his briefs and peeled them down his legs. Rory didn't protest; in fact, he spread his thighs so that I could easily remove the fabric. When my palm cupped Rory's fuzzy balls for the first time, we both moaned.

I ripped my lips from his, desperate to see every inch of my mate. I moaned again when I took in the sight of his pretty dick. Rory was just under six inches long and slim. The head of his dick was deep pink and glistening from the pre-cum that dripped out of him. Around his base and balls were covered in trimmed, shiny black hair.

"So gorgeous," I whispered, and Rory breathed a sigh of relief. I took his length in my hand and gave him a few slow pulls as he trembled against me. "You like that?"

"Yes!" he exclaimed, clawing at the top of my boxers. I pulled them down with one tug from my free hand and tossed them onto the floor. "Shit," Rory breathed, staring at my groin with wide eyes. I was nearly eight inches long and thick, and my base and heavy balls were coated in coarse brown hair. My wild and free side gave me a less tamed appearance than Rory, but he certainly didn't seem to mind.

I rolled on top of him, straddling his legs between mine and propping myself up on my elbows, keeping my weight off of his body. I rolled my hips and my mate cried out into the quiet room as our erections grinded together. "Is this okay?" I asked breathlessly. *I may die if he says no.*

"So...good..." Rory panted as I rocked my hips back and forth. We were both leaking steadily, slicking our skin and allowing our hard cocks to glide against one another. Each time I pivoted forward, our balls kissed together and sent electric shocks throughout my core.

I leaned in, careful not to put any pressure on Rory's body, and pressed my tongue to his right nipple, which was peaked from excitement. My mate keened and humped against me as I sucked his sensitive flesh into my mouth, flicking and swirling my tongue over its surface. When I bit down gently on the nub, Rory cried out and arched his back off of the mattress. He immediately hissed in pain and recoiled.

"I'm sorry," I said quickly, pulling my mouth from his nipple.

"No, it's not you; I felt so good, I forgot about my side. Please don't stop." I went back to my laving, but kept to easy flicks of my tongue and gentle kisses. Rory trembled and whimpered as I loved on his beautiful body. "Can...can you suck my neck again?"

I trailed open mouthed kisses up his chest and onto the opposite side of his throat than I marked earlier. "I love it when you tell me what you want," I whispered into his ear. I sucked the flesh behind his ear into my mouth and swallowed against it, drawing up another pretty purple love bite. Even if I couldn't give him my mating mark, I was still claiming him as my own.

I pushed my hips down, trapping our dicks between our stomachs and giving Rory even more sweet friction as I pistoned back and forth. I ground our flesh together; our balls rubbed and rolled against each other. I kissed the hickey on my mate's neck and pulled back, finding Rory's face was frozen in a look of pure ecstasy. His eyes were squinted shut behind his glasses. His mouth was parted slightly and his chest heaved with ragged breaths.

"Please don't stop, baby," Rory begged. My sweet mate was close.

"Not until you come for me," I promised. I humped against him faster as he cursed and keened at the ceiling. His fingers clutched the sheet at his sides and sweat beaded on his brow.

"Phoenix!" Rory's dick jerked against me and exploded, painting my lover's abdomen with burst after burst of thick, white liquid. I inhaled deeply, breathing the scent of my mate's pheromones and release into my lungs. It was the sweetest, most seductive thing I'd ever smelled. It brought me right to the edge.

"Oh, Rory," I moaned, snapping my hips faster. My balls rolled and lifted toward my body and I erupted. My cock pulsed as it shot my seed over Rory's stomach. Though I slowed my hips, I continued to rock against my mate's softening dick, milking every last drop from both of us.

Our mixed essence was almost too wonderful to bear. My hips stuttered to a stop and I sat up on my knees. I placed my fingers in our combined cum and massaged it into Rory's flesh, marking him with my scent as my wolf preened inside my mind.

"That was incredible," Rory whispered as he peeled his eyes open. He watched me curiously as I rubbed him down with our seed but didn't say anything. Not only was I beyond blessed to be my mate's first and only lover, I was lucky; if Rory had more experience, he'd probably find this to be an incredibly odd thing to do. But I couldn't help it; my body burned with the need to claim him.

"*You're* incredible," I countered and my sweet mate blushed. Two minutes ago he was begging me to suck his neck and make him come, but a simple compliment got him flustered. He was a treasure. I smiled once I was satisfied I got all of our scent rubbed into Rory's flesh.

"Would it be okay if I took that bath now?" he asked sweetly. "My ribs are pretty sore again. Don't get me wrong; that was totally worth it," he added quickly. "But soaking in some hot water sounds amazing."

Damn. A bath would surely wash away the scent I so lovingly and carefully marked him with, but I also knew it would help my mate feel better. "Of course." I leaned in and gave his lips and gentle peck. "I'll go run your water."

Chapter Six

Rory

Phoenix climbed off of the bed and unfortunately stepped back into his boxers before disappearing into the bathroom. Once he was out of the room, my mind went into overdrive.

Holy shit, I just had sex. Wait, does that count as sex? I should ask Dax. Oh my god, I have to tell Dax. He told me to bone that and I did! He'll be so proud of me! Damn, that felt good. I wonder how long I'll have to wait before we do that again. Phoenix's dick was huge! Would it hurt if he put it inside me? Does he even want that? I wonder how he feels about me. He said he really likes me and cares for me; could it ever be more? I've never felt about anyone how I feel for him. He's so sweet and wonderful and I can't stand the thought of being away from him. Holy shit, I think maybe I love him. Can you fall in love with someone so fast?

"Rory?" I flinched at the sound of Phoenix's voice and turned my head to find him grinning at me from the bathroom doorway. Apparently it wasn't the first time he tried getting my attention.

"Sorry," I muttered, feeling a blush take over my cheeks. "I was lost in thought."

His smile faltered. "Is everything okay?"

Shit. I didn't want him to think I was having regrets about what we did or something. "Everything's great," I promised and his grin returned.

"Good. Your water's ready; do you think you can make it by yourself?"

My head wasn't throbbing or spinning like it had been before, and I had some of Rowan's healing tea and food in my stomach to give me strength. I was sure I could make it across the room, but I wasn't about to miss out on the opportunity to touch my sexy boyfriend. *Holy shit, I have a sexy boyfriend!* That fact hadn't had a chance to settle in before now and it made my stomach flutter.

"I might need you to hold my hand." I tried to keep my voice as even and serious as possible, but Phoenix's smirk told me he wasn't buying it.

"Better safe than sorry," he winked.

"Exactly."

Phoenix chuckled as he came around to my side of the bed. He took my hands and slowly and carefully helped me onto my feet. "You look great," he smiled. "You're not shaking or getting pale like you did when you got up earlier."

I snorted a laugh as a funny thought struck me. Phoenix narrowed his eyes and cocked his head in confusion. "You *did* heal me with your dick," I explained, remembering Dax's words from earlier. Phoenix tipped his head back and laughed at the ceiling.

"You make me so happy, sweetheart." I beamed at him as he linked our fingers together and led me into the bathroom. "Here we go, nice and easy," he crooned as I stepped into the tub and lowered my body into the hot water. "How's the temperature?"

"Perfect." I sighed happily and slid further down into the bath. I rested my head against the wall of the tub and closed my eyes.

"Would you like me to give you some privacy?"

"You can stay. I mean, unless this is super weird or boring to just watch me soak in water."

Phoenix gave a quiet chuckle. "No way. I like just being with you."

I opened my eyes and smiled up at him. "Me too." I took a deep breath in through my nose and hummed. "It smells amazing in here. Is it the bath oil?"

"It's lavender. Rowan said it's supposed to be relaxing," he shrugged.

"How does he know so much about that kind of stuff?"

"He has a strong connection to nature and spent a lot of time learning from a very gifted healer."

"That's so cool. Do you think he would mind teaching me some stuff? I'd love to learn, but don't want to ask if you think I would bother him."

"I think he would love that," Phoenix smiled. "And you could never bother anyone. My friends really like you, Rory."

"I like them too." I sighed and let my eyes drift down Phoenix's incredible body. They lingered on the wolf inked onto his chest. "I love your tattoo. What does it mean?"

Phoenix gently pushed my hair off of my forehead. "Rowan, Stone and I have the same design. It symbolizes our unity together as friends and family. We look out for each other, help each other and care for each other."

"Like a wolf pack," I surmised, and Phoenix's smile widened as he nodded. "That's beautiful. I've always wanted a tattoo, but I'm too big of a weenie to actually get one. Did it hurt?"

"This one didn't," he shrugged again. "It felt like a warm tingle." He booped my nose with his finger. "And you're not a weenie, you hear me? You walked away from a terrible fall and are handling your injuries like a champ. You're braver and stronger than you give yourself credit for."

His words warmed me even more than the water surrounding me. "Thank you." I placed my hot, wet hand on top of his and Phoenix kissed the back of my knuckles.

I soaked in the tub until I was a shriveled prune. I would have gladly stayed there all day long, but the water grew cold. Phoenix helped me out of the basin and dried my skin with a fluffy towel. He led me back into the bedroom, where he presented me with the clothes he bought for me. I had dozens of comfortable outfits to choose from, and I wondered how long he was planning for me to stay with him. Not that I was about to question him; I didn't want to leave. I chose a pair of black sweatpants and a blue long-sleeved t-shirt. They fit me perfectly and felt great.

"You look lovely," Phoenix smiled. "What would you like to do, sweetheart? Do you need more rest? Or do you feel up to watching a movie or something?"

"I'd love to watch a movie, but would it be okay if I called Dax first? He'll be going to work soon and I'd like to check in with him; let him know I'm doing better."

"Of course." He retrieved the phone from the wall and handed it to me. "I'll be in the living room."

"Thanks." I would have asked him to stay, but I wanted to fill my best friend in on my afternoon and thought I'd be too shy to do it with Phoenix sitting right beside me.

Phoenix grabbed the tray of food scraps and my empty mug from the nightstand before disappearing from the bedroom, shutting the door behind him. I dialed Dax's number and he answered on the second ring.

"Oh god, he's worse isn't he? I'm on my way."

"No Dax, it's me. And I'm actually feeling better."

"Thank goodness," he sighed. "Jeez, you scared me. You can't do that; with my cholesterol, I'm a ticking time bomb!"

"Sorry."

"It's okay." Dax let out a long breath. "So you're feeling better, huh? That's great!"

"Yeah, Phoenix's friend Rowan made me some herbal tea and ointment to help my injuries. I'm not one hundred percent yet, of course, but I'm feeling pretty good."

"Ointment? Did you get Mr. Hot Ranger to rub it all over you?"

"Maaaybe," I drawled, wearing a naughty grin even though he couldn't see it.

"*What?* I need details. Now."

I chuckled at my crazy friend, though his nosiness didn't surprise me. We told each other everything. "He's been taking such good care of me, Dax. He carried me to the bathroom and made me lunch and drew me a bath. He even bought me a bunch of clothes so I'd be comfortable while I heal."

"Aw, he sounds great, but I meant I wanted *dirty* details. Please tell me you slept with him."

"Kind of."

"Oh. My. Gawd. I was just joking, but you seriously did?"

"Well, like I said...kind of. We didn't actually have sex, but we did get naked and...rubbed our things together."

Dax was quiet for a moment before bursting into laughter. "Rubbed our things together!" he repeated through snickers. "You are too freaking cute." It took a minute for him to calm down. "Ugh, I'm so jealous. That's more action than I've seen in months."

"Wait; you and Justin live together. Why haven't you done it in months?"

"It's...complicated." He cleared his throat. "But that's not interesting. I want to talk about your news." I was confused about Dax's situation, but I was also beyond okay with not discussing his and Justin's sex life. "So how was it?"

"Incredible," I sighed. "It felt so good and Phoenix is *huge!* And he made sure I was comfortable with everything and that he didn't hurt my injuries. He's so strong and tough but he's gentle and sweet with me at the same time. He's just amazing, Dax."

"Sounds like you really like him."

"I think it's more than that," I admitted. "I think I'm falling in love with him." Dax gasped at the same time a crashing sound came from the other side of the bedroom door. I covered the mouthpiece on the phone and called out, "Are you okay?" to Phoenix.

"Yeah, I'm fine. I just dropped a plate in the kitchen," he called back.

"You don't think I'm crazy, do you?" I asked Dax. "I mean, I haven't known him long and I *did* hit my head pretty hard. Do you think I'm just confused?" A pained whimper cut through the air. *Does Phoenix have a dog?* I loved dogs and couldn't wait to get my hands on it. *Oh, I hope the little sweetie didn't cut its paw on the smashed plate.*

"I think you're just nervous," Dax replied, drawing my attention back to our conversation. "You've got a good head on your shoulders and you've always been able to get a good read on people. If you feel love for him, I'm sure it's legit. Don't get in your own head and doubt yourself." He sighed. "Just don't forget about me when you're spending all of your time rubbing dicks with the hot ranger."

I snorted a laugh. "I could never forget about you. Besides, I can't spend *all* of my time here. Once I'm completely healed, I'll have to come home." The thought made my chest ache and I heard another whimper from the house.

"*Or*, you could slowly move your things in and hope he doesn't notice," Dax suggested. *That might work. I've got plenty of clothes here now, so I wouldn't have to worry about that. I could just bring in a few things at a time so it wouldn't be too obvious.* Dax laughed out loud. "Oh my god, you're actually thinking about it, aren't you? That was a joke." *Oh, right...a joke. I guess it would be a little invasive.* "Listen, I've got to get ready for work, but thanks for calling. I'm so glad you're getting better. Good luck with your man and call again soon, okay? Love you."

"Love you too."

I clicked off the call and dialed my boss from the grocery store. I told him about my injuries and that I'd need some time off. He reminded me that the time off would be unpaid and informed me if I didn't return to work within 21 days, I'd forfeit my position. Not that it'd be a great loss, but I *did* need the money.

I returned the phone and shuffled across the room to the door, noting the slight tenderness on my right side. All in all, though, I didn't feel too bad, and I was tired of lying in bed. I opened the bedroom door and took a look around the rest of Phoenix's house.

The living room and kitchen were joined in one large, open area. The wooden floors and walls gave the home a warm, welcoming feel, as did the fireplace crackling in the corner. The kitchen was clean and filled with shiny stainless steel appliances and cabinets that matched the other wood in the house and looked handmade. The living room held a comfortable-looking sofa and chair, coffee table and TV. There was a large rug with a hunter green and maroon design that tied everything together beautifully.

"Look at you, sweetheart," Phoenix said with a smile as he came in through the front door. "You look great."

"Thanks. Were you taking the dog out?"

"No, I was just talking to Stone for a..." Phoenix's brows tucked in with confusion. "What dog?"

"I thought I heard a dog whining earlier. Do you have one?"

"Oh, um..." Phoenix scratched the back of his head, looking away. "No, I don't have a dog. Maybe you heard something outside? We have all kinds of wildlife here."

"Yeah, that's probably it." *Damn*.

"Do you like dogs?"

"Love them. I had a chocolate lab named Duke when I was growing up. We were inseparable and it broke my heart when he died. I've always wanted another one, but my apartment building doesn't allow pets."

"I'm sorry."

"Eh, maybe one day," I shrugged. "I was just looking at your house; it's gorgeous."

"I'm so glad you like it. Rowan, Stone and I built all three of our homes together."

"You *built* this?" I took another look around with a newfound appreciation for the craftsmanship. "Holy cow, I'm impressed. I can't even figure out Lego sets."

Phoenix chuckled as he stepped beside me and wrapped an arm around my shoulders. "Everyone has their own talents. I'd love to hear about what you enjoy." He led me over to the sofa and sat down beside me.

"I love photography. That's actually why I was here in the state park to begin with. I just bought a new..." My stomach sank. I'd been so focused on Phoenix and my fall I forgot all about my camera. "You didn't happen to find a camera where I fell, did you?" Phoenix's sad smile dashed any hope I held.

"Rowan and Stone searched the area after we rescued you. They did find your camera, but I'm sorry to say it was smashed by the rocks."

"Damn." My heart broke over the beautiful photographs I lost, along with all of the money I spent. "I know it's stupid to be so upset over it; I could have died, but I saved up for a long time to get it."

"It's not stupid," Phoenix insisted. "It meant a lot to you. But I think I may have something to cheer you up." He rose from the couch and walked into the kitchen. He pulled something from one of the cabinets and returned to me, presenting a box with a wide smile. My breath caught at the sight of the exact same camera that got busted.

"You bought this for me?" I whispered, roving my eyes over the gift. I knew it wasn't cheap; but Phoenix spending quite a bit of money on me wasn't as touching as the fact that he wanted to buy this for me just to make me happy.

He sat next to me again. "I was thinking once you feel up to it, I'd like to take you out on some trails so you can get as many photos as you like. My friends and I even have some paths we've made ourselves. They're further away from the ones that the public travels, so the chance of seeing animals is higher due to less foot traffic to scare them."

"I don't know what to say." I placed the camera box on the coffee table and wrapped my arms around Phoenix's neck. "Thank you."

"You're welcome." He gently wrapped his arms around my waist and drew circles on my lower back with his fingertips. His touch was warm and comforting. Being near him just felt...right.

I pulled back until our noses were nearly touching. I combed my fingers through his short hair and inhaled his sweet breath that fanned across my face. I looked into his eyes and my breath caught; they got more intense and captivating each time I saw them. My face inched closer to his, pulled by an invisible force that I didn't want to fight.

Our gazes remained locked until the very moment our lips touched. My eyes drifted closed and a quiet whimper escaped me as Phoenix kissed me softly. His lips devoured mine and I opened readily to invite him in. Our tongues glided across one another and I moaned at our sweet mixture of flavors.

I jumped away from Phoenix when a knock sounded on the front door. My boyfriend blew out a long breath and gave me a tight smile before rising to answer it.

*****

Phoenix

I held in a growl as I stepped to the door, silently cursing whoever was on the other side. They were interrupting my time with my mate; time I wanted to use to secure our bond. Any animosity I held melted away at the sight of Rowan on my doorstep, holding a teapot and wearing a wide smile.

"Hey, Alpha. I came by to bring Rory some more tea and check up on him," he said as I pulled the door open.

"Alpha?" Rory asked from behind us. Rowan's eyes widened with worry. "That's a fun nickname." I looked to my mate to see him standing up from the sofa. "How did you get it?" He stepped beside me and nuzzled against me. I happily wrapped my arm around his shoulders, pleased Rory was comfortable with showing affection in front of my friend.

"Phoenix has always been kind of the leader of our little group," Rowan answered, still looking nervous.

"Aw, you guys really are like a wolf pack," Rory smiled. Rowan's eyes snapped to mine and I gave a subtle shake of my head.

"He saw my tattoo," I explained.

"Of course," Rowan nodded. He cleared his throat. "So Rory, you look like you're feeling much better."

"I am, thank you. Your treatments are working wonders."

"Great. I brought you some more tea; I figured you would be out."

"Oh, come on in and put it down," Rory offered, holding a hand out toward the kitchen. "Thanks a lot. Hey, Phoenix and I were getting ready to watch a movie. Would you like to join us?" My mate flinched and looked at me worriedly. "Sorry, I mean...if that's okay with you. I don't know what came over me."

"Don't be sorry. I want you to think of this as your home, sweetheart." In my mind, it already was, and I hoped soon Rory would feel that way as well. Rory gave me a sweet smile and lurched up onto his tiptoes to kiss my cheek. Rowan's answering grin was blinding.

"If you're sure I won't be intruding..." Rowan asked, looking between us.

"Not at all," I shrugged. I wanted my friends and my mate to spend time together; they'd be together for eternity, after all. Rowan entered and placed the teapot on my stovetop before sitting on the sofa. I poured a mug of tea for my mate and he sipped it greedily.

"Would Stone like to watch with us?" Rory asked sweetly.

"Tonight is Stone's shift on patrol," Rowan answered and Rory cocked his head in confusion. "We take turns monitoring the area for lost tourists or problems with the trails."

"Well thank goodness for that or I'd be coyote food," Rory answered. My chest ached at the possibilities if I hadn't found him. "So what types of movies do you like, Row?"

Rowan's gaze snapped to mine at the nickname, obviously judging for my reaction. I just smiled; I was happy Rory was comfortable around my friend and that they were getting along. "I like all kinds, but horror movies are my favorite."

Rory shuddered. "Not me; those things creep me out. My friend Dax loves them, though, and makes me watch them with him sometimes. Last time he did, I got so worked up, I made him sleep in bed with me afterward. He thought it was hilarious, but I had nightmares for a week about that damn clown and his stupid red balloon."

Rowan laughed at my sweet mate's story. "Now *that* was a good movie." Rory made a disgusted face and made my friend laugh harder.

"Okay, so scary movies are out," I chuckled, bringing up the movie list on my

TV. I handed the remote to Rory. "Pick whatever you like, sweetheart."

I smiled as he scrolled through the selections with a determined face, taking his duty very seriously. His eyes popped open as he turned to me and I thought he'd found his pick, but he asked, "Do you have popcorn?"

"Hmm, I think so." I went to the kitchen and rifled through my cabinets until I found a jar of popping corn. "Here we go."

"Awesome. We can't have a movie without popcorn," Rory insisted seriously. "I've never seen that kind, though; I usually just get the bags you throw in the microwave. Can I watch you pop it?"

"Of course." Rory and Rowan both rose from the sofa to join me in the kitchen. My mate watched with rapt attention as I filled a pot with oil and heated the kernels over the heat of the stovetop.

"This is so cool," he said as the kernels burst. He blushed as he looked between Rowan and me. "Sorry...it doesn't take much to entertain me, I guess."

"I think it's adorable," I assured before pecking his lips. Rowan's smile told me he felt the same way.

After I transferred the popcorn into a large bowl, Rory melted some butter in the microwave and poured it on top until the kernels were little soggy balls of mush. He then sprinkled on enough salt to rival a blizzard. "Mm, that's perfect," he moaned as he popped a piece into his mouth to test it. He fed me a kernel and my teeth curled at the saltiness, but I plastered a smile onto my face.

"Delicious." Rory grabbed the bowl and proudly marched to the sofa as Rowan chuckled at the way my eye twitched at the sour flavor. I made a mental note to buy microwavable popcorn that Rory wouldn't need to doctor up the next time I went to town.

I sat next to my mate on the sofa and Rowan pointed to my beloved recliner, raising his eyebrows in question. I nodded my permission and he smiled as he sank himself into my favorite spot. At least he asked; Stone plopped his ass in it every chance he got just to irritate me.

"Is this movie okay?" Rory asked as he pointed to the screen. A picture was displayed of several men who appeared to be spies. They were dressed in suits and held an array of weapons. "I love action films."

"Me too," I smiled.

Rory pressed play and settled into my side as we watched mysterious plots unfurl and dramatic fight scenes play out. My mate chomped away on his popcorn, thankfully not noticing that Rowan and I didn't touch it. He gasped at each explosion and flinched during all of the gunfire. Though he seemed thoroughly immersed in the film, Rory only made it about halfway through before he was snoozing on my shoulder.

"He'll get tired more often until he's fully healed," Rowan explained once the movie ended and I turned off the television. "He looks great, though; he's healing more quickly than I imagined."

"Of course he is," I replied proudly. "He is the Alpha's mate; he's destined to be tough." I ran my fingers through Rory's hair and smiled down at him. He was so much more than tough; he was also sweet, tender, strong and caring. He was everything I could ever ask for.

"I'm happy to see you two getting so close," he said with a wistful smile on his face. "May I ask what became of his other relationship you mentioned?"

"It was just a misunderstanding. He was speaking of a friend, not a lover."

"I knew everything would work out." Rowan rose from the chair and stepped toward the front door. "I'll let you settle down for the evening. Thanks for allowing me to spend some time with your mate; he is truly a gift."

I gave my friend a smile and nod, and he left my home, quietly closing the door behind him as to not disturb Rory. I scooped my sleeping love into my arms and carefully carried him into the bedroom. I settled him on the mattress and tucked the blankets around him. After returning to the kitchen to tidy up the popcorn mess and then checking the fireplace to make sure it was safe for the night, I stripped down to my underwear and took my place in bed next to Rory.

He instinctively snuggled closer to me, drawing a tender smile to my face. I took his glasses from his nose and placed them safely on the nightstand before wrapping my arms around his body.

"Goodnight, sweet Rory," I whispered into his ear. I gently kissed his cheek and he let out a quiet moan.

"Night," he mumbled back, sending a waft of buttery breath in my direction. "Love you."

My heart stammered in my chest. I'd overheard Rory telling his friend earlier that he thought he could be falling in love with me, but to hear the declaration made me happier than words can describe. My mate was whispering to me in his slumber, but I knew the words to be true. They echoed my own feelings for him.

"I love you too," I whispered, but my mate was fast asleep.

Chapter Seven

Rory

"Rory?" a faraway voice called to me. "Sweetheart, I made you some breakfast."

I blinked my eyes until they (mostly) focused on a smiling Phoenix holding a plate of food. I grabbed my glasses from the nightstand and shoved them on. "I fell asleep during the movie, didn't I?" I remembered finishing the popcorn and snuggling up to Phoenix and then...it was all blank.

"Yeah, but that's okay; we can watch it again later if you want."

"Rowan didn't think I was rude, did he?" I asked as Phoenix settled into bed next to me.

"Of course not. He knows you'll be sleepy until you're fully healed. He said you're looking great, though."

"Aw, that was nice of him." I smiled as I took the plate Phoenix held out to me, which held scrambled eggs, bacon and toast. "This looks incredible, baby. Thank you." I got a thrill from calling my boyfriend the name, and his smile said he liked it as well. Phoenix leaned in and gave me a quick kiss. I tasted the subtle flavor of mint toothpaste on his lips and I flinched.

"What's wrong?"

"I just realized my mouth probably tastes like buttery butt."

Phoenix laughed out loud even though I wasn't joking. "I love your sense of humor." I thanked him even though again, I was totally serious; especially now as I got a good taste of my mouth and confirmed that yep, it was rank. "And I promise it doesn't, but I've got a toothbrush in the bathroom for you. I didn't want to wake you last night."

"Great. I'll smash these eggs and then go freshen up." Phoenix chuckled again and we tucked into our breakfast, which was delicious. My man was a great cook.

"Actually, after we eat, would you mind if I take a shower?"

"Rory, you don't have to ask me for my permission for anything," Phoenix replied with a gentle smile. "I told you I want you to think of this as your home and I meant it. You're welcome to do anything you wish. And actually, a shower sounds great. I was thinking of taking one myself."

"You can go first," I offered. This was the man's house, after all; no matter what he said, I didn't want to be rude.

"I was thinking perhaps we could take one together."

Oh, sweet mercy. My morning wood had just started to deflate, but Phoenix's suggestion plumped it right back up. I tried to keep my voice even when I answered, "That sounds nice," but I couldn't hide the huskiness to my tone. The man was just too sexy. He winked at me and bit into his toast.

My hands trembled with anticipation as I ate the rest of my breakfast. They shook so hard I dropped my toast, smearing jelly all down the front of my shirt, but Phoenix didn't mention anything. I was sure he noticed, but he was a gentleman.

"All finished?" he asked once I'd cleared my plate.

"Yes and thanks again, that was great."

"You're very welcome." He kissed my cheek and took the plate from my hands. "I'll take these into the kitchen and then start our shower."

Once Phoenix left the room, I scurried to the bathroom, noticing my ribs felt much better, and my head didn't hurt at all. I pissed the best I could with the stiffy between my legs and whipped off my shirt, tossing the evidence of the jelly smear into the clothes hamper. I caught sight of myself in the mirror, noticing the faint green and yellow blotches that covered my right side. The bruises weren't nearly as bad as I'd imagined they'd be.

I washed my hands and searched the medicine cabinet, finding the extra toothbrush Phoenix mentioned. He entered the room just as I was rinsing out my mouth.

"Well isn't this a sexy surprise?" Phoenix said as he stepped behind me. He wrapped his arms around my waist and kissed a line up my neck and behind my ear. He nipped the hickey he left yesterday afternoon and I moaned aloud. "Mm, I love this beautiful body." His hands roamed my stomach and chest, gently caressing over my smooth skin. I'd never felt beautiful until I met Phoenix, but he made me believe it.

"I don't think this is very fair," I pouted and Phoenix lifted his mouth from my throat, giving me a confused look in the reflection of the mirror. "I'm half naked and you're fully dressed. I want to see *your* beautiful body too."

"You're right, it's only fair," he teased. He took a step away from me and made a show of slowly removing his shirt. I held back a moan at the sight of his toned body and his powerful tattoo as he raised the fabric over his head. "There we go; even."

"But we can't get in the shower like this. What should we do about that?" I wanted to spin around and rip his clothes off of him, but our playful teasing only added to the intensity and excitement of the moment.

Phoenix stepped closer to me again. "Hmm, I think we better get rid of these." He slipped his fingertips inside the waistband of my pants. "We wouldn't want them to get wet." Too late for that; my weeping dick was soaking their front, but I kept that tidbit to myself. He pushed the fabric over the swell of my ass and it pooled around my feet. "Much better."

"Not quite." I tucked my hands behind me and unsnapped the button of Phoenix's jeans. As I lowered the zipper, a firm length pressed against my fingers. I gripped the sides of his pants and pulled them along with his boxers to the ground. His dick slapped against my back with a *thud* and we both moaned.

"Oh, Rory," Phoenix groaned as his hands snaked back around to my front. "You don't know what you do to me, sweetheart." I had a pretty good idea, and the evidence was jutting out in front of me. One of my lover's hands slid down my abdomen and cupped my fuzzy balls. He squeezed gently and I whimpered as I rested my head back onto his chest. "You like that?"

"I love everything you do to me," I answered honestly. Phoenix was a master with his hands, whether he was gently caring for my injuries or making my body sing. I wanted anything and everything he was willing to give.

"And I love doing it." Phoenix pressed his erection to my back, painting my spine with a line of pre-cum. "Feel how hard you make me?" I cried out as he rocked his hips back and forth, rubbing his dick against my flesh. "Can I make you feel good, Rory?"

"Yes!" I begged as my chest heaved with ragged breaths. I didn't know *how* he wanted to make me feel good, but I also didn't care. I was ready for everything with him, and I trusted him wholeheartedly to never hurt me.

Phoenix hummed as his other hand slid down my body and wrapped around the base of my dick. "Oh, I'm gonna make you feel so good, sweetheart." He bent his knees just enough to settle his cock in the crack of my ass. He gave my dick a long, slow pull as he grinded his length against me.

"Ohhh god," I drawled, letting my eyes slide closed and giving myself over to the sensation of his touch.

"That's it, Rory," Phoenix crooned. "Relax into me. I'll take care of you." He stroked my dick faster as he undulated back and forth, riding the crevice between my cheeks. My cock leaked steadily as he pumped it, allowing his palm to glide easily against my skin. Phoenix massaged my balls and gingerly pulled them, sending sparks of heat up into my pelvis.

Pressure burned and bloomed inside me. My release was close, but I wanted this to last as long as possible. I bit down on my bottom lip and focused on my breathing. Phoenix pressed closer to me and his cock nestled further into my crack. I screamed when his heated flesh rubbed against my pucker.

"You like that?" Phoenix panted, rocking into me furiously while jacking me just as fast. I nodded quickly against his chest. Words evaded me as I soaked up the feeling of his skin on mine. "One day I'm gonna be inside this tight little hole," he grunted and I couldn't hold back anymore.

My balls lifted and rolled. My eyes slammed shut and I cried out, erupting over Phoenix's fingers and into the sink. He didn't stop stroking me, and milked out every last drop I had to give. My knees grew weak and I gripped the sides of the sink for support.

"I've got you." Phoenix released my cock and wrapped his arms around my waist to support my weight. I felt his chest heaving against my back as he rubbed against me. "Oh god," he cried, humping faster. "Rory!" His dick jerked against me and wet heat splattered up my back. It trickled down my cheeks and into my crack. I moaned as it slid over my sensitive hole.

Phoenix kissed my neck again, this time with an open mouth and lazy strokes of his tongue. His breath was hot against my skin as it slowed from pants to a deep, even pattern. "Are you okay?" he finally whispered. "I didn't hurt you, did I?"

"No," I answered quickly. "You didn't hurt me. That was incredible, baby."

He hummed his agreement and kissed my neck once more before stepping back. Phoenix placed his hands on my lower back and just as he did the last time we were together, massaged his cum into my skin. It was a little odd, but somehow comforting. His touch felt nice and I'd never turn down extra attention from him. The way he rubbed his seed into me reminded me of an animal marking its territory, which brought a smile to my lips.

"You have a beautiful smile," Phoenix said dreamily. His reflection in the mirror showed his own goofy grin. "What are you thinking about?"

"I was thinking how nice that feels." I gave a slight chuckle. "And how it's like you're marking me."

Phoenix's hands stilled. "How do you feel about that?" I couldn't read the expression on his face.

"I *want* you to mark me." Phoenix's eyes darkened and his fingertips dug into my flesh. "Actually, I think you already did." I tipped my head to the side, showing off the string of hickeys that painted my throat.

"I love seeing my marks on you." His voice was husky and his gaze intense. My spent dick gave a valiant twitch, but it was too well loved to rise again so soon.

"Me too."

Phoenix's eyes trailed down to my throat and he licked his lips. I lay my head on my shoulder, giving him access to my neck. I'd never turn down more of his love bites. His breathing was heavy as his mouth inched closer to my skin. Just before he made contact, however, he closed his eyes and took a deep breath. He kissed my neck gently and stepped away. I wasn't sure what happened, but figured maybe he was too spent as well to get all worked up again.

"Rory, after our shower, would you feel up to a walk in the woods? There's something I'd really like to show you."

"That sounds great," I beamed. "I'm feeling pretty good and I'd love to take some pictures on those trails you were talking about."

"Perfect." He leaned in and pecked my cheek. "I'll start our water."

While he did that, I rinsed the mess I'd sprayed in the sink down the drain and placed my glasses on the edge of the basin. When I turned towards Phoenix, he offered me his hand and helped me into the shower.

We took turns washing each other's bodies with his crisp, sporty body wash. It smelled great, but I was confused; Phoenix always smelled woodsy and earthy. Nothing like his soap; it was a hundred times better. I shrugged off my question, chalking the scent up to his cologne or something.

Phoenix's hands were gentle and thorough as they cleansed me. It amazed me how he could go from insanely sexy and commanding as he drove my body to pleasure, to tender and caring in the blink of an eye. There were so many layers to him and I loved them all.

After speaking to Dax and spending more time with Phoenix, I was positive about my feelings for him. It was quick, but it was true. Something about this man called out to me and I couldn't help but answer. It felt as if I'd known him forever; like he was the piece of myself I didn't know I was missing until I met him. Now I couldn't imagine my life without him. I needed him. I needed to be with him.

Phoenix left me to my thoughts as he rinsed my body and helped me out of the shower. He dried me off and I did the same for him. I wanted to care for him the way he took care of me. I ran a comb through my mostly dry locks, donned my glasses and followed Phoenix back into the bedroom.

"We should probably put some of this on you before we head out," he said, holding up the little pot of ointment. "It's a bit of a walk and I don't want you getting sore. But if you *do* get sore, tell me and I'll carry you, okay? Don't push yourself too hard."

"You're the best, you know that?"

"I try," he shrugged and I laughed at my silly man. He winked and crooked his finger, beckoning me to come closer. I stood toe to toe with him as he slathered my side and temples with the cream. It still burned a bit, but I'd gotten used to it. Plus, it helped my pain tremendously, so I didn't mind.

Once Phoenix was satisfied I was adequately covered in tingly goop, he dressed in jeans, a red and black plaid flannel shirt, and brown hiking boots. With his strong body and scruffy beard, he looked every bit the part of a sexy mountain man.

I looked every bit the nerd as I pulled on my freshly cleaned skinny jeans and a black sweatshirt that matched my glasses. Phoenix squished his lips to the side as he watched me lace up my sneakers.

"I'm sorry, sweetheart, I didn't think to get you any hiking boots. I'll buy you some next time we go to town. You'll need them for the trails; I don't want you slipping again." I stood up straight and he pecked my lips. "Plus, when winter comes, you'll want something to keep your toes warm. The elevations get quite a bit of snow."

My heart pounded at his words. He was envisioning me being here for quite some time. Even if he meant when I visited him instead of physically staying here, it didn't matter. When he pictured his future, he saw me in it.

"Thank you," I told him when I realized I hadn't said anything.

"Of course," he smiled. "I promised to always take care of you." My pulse quickened even more at the word 'always'. He held his hand out for me to take. "Ready?"

I linked my fingers in his and smiled. "Ready."

Chapter Eight

Rory

"You weren't kidding about the wildlife on these trails," I whispered to Phoenix as I snapped a picture of a wild hare in the distance. I'd already gotten photos of many different birds, another doe and several squirrels. The new shots eased the pain of losing my first ones.

"You're really good at that," he whispered back, looking at the digital screen over my shoulder. "It's a beautiful photo."

"The camera does most of the work," I shrugged.

"No way; you have talent," he argued. "And you light up when you're taking pictures. It's a pleasure to watch."

My cheeks flushed. "Thank you. It's something I've always enjoyed." Phoenix leaned in and gave me a kiss. At the sound of our lips smacking, the hare bounced away. "Aw, bye bunny. Thanks for posing for me!"

Phoenix chuckled. "You're too cute."

He took my hand and led me further down the path. It wasn't as clear as the ones meant for the public; the trail was a bit overgrown, but the earth was flat. There were no hills or uneven ground to hurt my side, and the scenery couldn't be beat. Not only was there plenty of wildlife, but pretty plants lined the path and the trees were tall and lush.

"Baby, could I take a few photos of you?" I asked hopefully. I'd gotten my fill of flora and fauna. I wanted some shots of the gorgeous man at my side.

"If it will make you happy, you got it. Where do you want me?"

"Hmm…" I looked around the area for the best backdrop. "Lean against that tree." Phoenix propped his elbow on the tree and rested his head on his hand. "Okay, give me a smile." He did as I asked and I snapped several photos. "Oh, that's gorgeous. Okay now give me a sultry look." He tucked his bottom lip between his teeth and popped a few buttons of his shirt while I took a string of photographs. "Oh my."

Phoenix tipped his head back and laughed. I snapped quickly to capture the beautiful moment. "You like that, sweetheart?" He undid the last few buttons of his shirt and slid it off of his shoulders.

"Oh, that's nice." Phoenix struck several poses as I greedily caught the images. He unbuttoned his jeans and I smiled widely. "I like where this is going." He pushed his jeans and underwear down so that the deep cut 'V' of his pelvis showed, along with the top of his pubic hair. "Good lord, you're sexy."

I took several photos of his front, and then his back when he turned around and playfully stuck his ass out of the top of his jeans. I had a feeling I'd be revisiting these photographs often.

"Have you captured my good side?" Phoenix asked, shaking his butt at me.

"They're all good sides," I insisted and he chuckled again. "The only thing that'd make it better is if you took *all* your clothes off." I played it off as a joke, but I definitely wouldn't complain if he took me up on my offer.

"I will in a minute," he promised, and my heart rate sped up. "But first, I want to talk to you about something." He buttoned his jeans and his expression grew serious.

"Is something wrong?"

"No, but it *is* important." I lowered my camera to my side, giving him my full attention. Phoenix cupped both of my cheeks in his large, warm palms. His enchanting green eyes looked right into me as he took a deep breath. "I love you, Rory."

My heart skipped a beat and my mouth went dry. "I love you too," I whispered, unable to speak louder. Phoenix gave me a beautiful smile and my nerves subsided enough to allow me to voice the rest of my thoughts. "I was afraid to say anything so soon, but almost since the moment I met you, I've felt this pull toward you. It's like you complete me and I can't live without you."

"I feel the same way, and there's a reason for it." He took another deep breath. "All their lives, shifters know that Fate will grant them their one true mate. The one person who will complete them. The one they will love and cherish for all time. They know by scent and instinct when they've met their mate. I knew when I met you that you were mine; my fated mate, my true love, my forever."

"That's beautiful," I whispered. "I believe you're my true love too. But...what is a shifter? I don't understand."

"Shifters have been around since the beginning of time, but fear and misunderstanding of our kind forced us to hide from those who hunted us and wanted to rid us from the earth. They found us unnatural and dangerous; feral, even. So, we withdrew from the public and formed packs. We stayed with our own kind; plus our mates, of course. Over time, we began integrating back into the public eye, but kept our identities hidden. Most people have never heard of us or our heritage."

"I'm sorry your people went through that," I replied sadly. Nobody deserved to be hunted like animals just because they were different. "But I'm afraid I still don't understand what you're saying. Is 'shifter' a religion?" It wouldn't be the first time a group was persecuted. Phoenix had mentioned a strong connection to nature and healers; maybe shifters were like wiccans?

"No, sweetheart." Phoenix gave me a gentle smile and ran his fingers through my hair. "Shifters are immortal beings. We have a human side as well as an animal side. We can shift between forms at will, and have total control no matter what form we take. My other form is a wolf."

I blinked at him. "Um...okay." My poor man was delusional. But I wouldn't give up on him. I loved him; I'd get him help.

"It's the truth," he insisted, looking desperate. "Rowan and Stone are wolves too. They're my pack and I'm their leader. That's why Rowan called me Alpha. That's what the tattoo is about." Phoenix pointed to the wolf on his chest. "It's not an actual tattoo; it's part of our bodies. When we formed our own pack and pledged our alliance, the design appeared on our skin and linked us together." His body deflated. "You don't believe me, do you?"

I set my camera on the ground and took both of his hands in mine. "I believe that *you* believe it. I don't know where these ideas came from, but I'm not judging, baby. I love you. We'll figure this out."

"I was afraid of this," Phoenix said, releasing one of my hands to run his fingers through his scruffy beard. "Remember when I said I wanted to bring you out here to show you something?" I nodded. "It wasn't just the trails and the scenery. I want to show you my wolf form."

I sighed as he took a few steps back from me. My heart broke for him as he removed the remainder of his clothing. I wondered if he'd act like a wolf in front of me or if he'd get upset when his delusions didn't play out. Either way, I'd support him the best I could.

"Remember, you don't have to be afraid when I'm in my wolf form. I'm still me. I'm in control and I would never hurt you. I can understand you, but I can't speak." I gave him a tight smile and a nod, preparing myself for whatever shit show was about to go down.

Crackling and popping sounds filled the air, but Phoenix and I were both standing still. We weren't stepping on twigs and there was no one around us. It took a minute for me to realize the noises were coming from his body; his body which was contorting and sprouting thick brown fur in front of my eyes.

My brain screamed for me to run from the scene in front of me, but my heart held my feet firm. My eyes widened at the sight of my boyfriend bending and reshaping until a large, powerful wolf stood before me. *Okay, so he's not crazy. Unless Rowan put some hallucinogens in that special tea of his and I'm living the same fantasy.* But when I searched my soul, I knew I could trust what my eyes beheld.

The animal didn't advance toward me. It tucked its ears back in a non-threatening manner and lowered its tail. Its beautiful emerald eyes stared straight into mine, but they weren't intimidating. They were begging for understanding and acceptance. *I'd know those eyes anywhere.*

"Phoenix?" I asked in a shaky whisper. The wolf tipped its head down in a nod. My

legs could no longer support me and I
dropped to my knees in front of the animal.
"I'm so sorry I doubted you. It's just...this
is...wow." I couldn't come up with any
intelligent words to describe the confusion
and amazement I felt.

"You're beautiful." I'd never seen a
more majestic and magnificent animal. *Wait.*
I gasped as realization dawned on me. "You
were like this when you found me, weren't
you?" Phoenix nodded again. "I remember
seeing a pretty wolf after I fell, but I thought
I imagined the whole thing; that a wolf
would have eaten me." Phoenix whimpered
and I gasped again. "It was you I heard at
the house." Somehow this crazy situation
was starting to make sense.

I raised a trembling hand toward his
head, reminding myself that this was
Phoenix and that he wouldn't hurt me. Still,
it seemed polite to ask, "Can I pet you?" He
answered by nuzzling his face against my
open palm. I ran my hand over his head and

scratched behind his ears, noting the way his tail wagged behind him. "You like that, don't you?" I chuckled and Phoenix chuffed a sound that almost sounded like a laugh.

"This is incredible." I shook my head and an idea hit me. "Can I take your picture?" Phoenix stepped back and struck a pose, pushing out his chest and lifting his head high, making me laugh again. "You're a ham no matter *what* form you're in." It amazed me how easily that rolled off of my tongue; how easy my mind accepted the events. But, I'd seen the shift with my own eyes, so it was hard to refute.

I grabbed my camera from the ground and stood, circling Phoenix and capturing images of him from every angle. Once I was satisfied, I dropped to my knees again and set my camera aside. "You are the perfect muse." I buried my fingers into the wiry hair on his back, and Phoenix surprised me by licking a wet line up my cheek. I chuckled as I wiped the wolf spit from my face.

"Thank you for trusting me with this. You know, it's pretty cool that my boyfriend is a badass wolf." I scratched behind his ears again and smiled at the way his tongue lolled out of his mouth. He didn't look so badass at the moment, but I could tell from his size and structure it was true. "I'll admit it was a shock at first, but honestly it doesn't matter to me what you are; man, shifter...I love *you*." I kissed his cold, wet nose and within moments, a naked, human Phoenix crouched before me.

He wrapped his arms around my shoulders and pulled me tightly against his body. "Thank you, Rory," he whispered into my ear. "For accepting and loving me."

"You make it easy," I replied, rolling my eyes at myself and how cheesy I sounded.

"There's still so much I need to tell you about my family, my culture and what it means to be my mate. I want to take you home where you will be comfortable and warm for us to talk." It didn't escape me how easily Phoenix referred to his home as mine too. I wondered if that was part of the mate stuff he needed to speak to me about. But it didn't frighten or worry me. I was excited to hear more about this incredible turn of events and the remarkable man before me.

"I'd love that."

Chapter Nine
Phoenix

I settled my mate onto the sofa and made sure he was comfortable. Though he didn't appear to be in any pain, I poured him a mug of Rowan's tea. Rory took it with a smile and sipped the warm liquid as I gathered my thoughts, trying to decide the best way to begin this conversation.

"So," Rory began, "You said your father taught you how to be a good leader. Was he an Alpha too?"

I smiled at how receptive and intelligent my mate was. "He was. He was the leader of the pack I was born into. My mother was his fated match and ruled by his side as the Alpha mate." I went into detail about my brother, how he betrayed our father and took over the pack by force. As I described to Rory how my friends fled with me and created our own pack, his face fell.

"You lost your whole family in one day," he replied sadly. "I'm so sorry." He took my hand and squeezed it gently.

"Thank you. It was many years ago, but it still hurts. Though I was always meant to leave my old pack to lead my own, shifters forge deep and lasting bonds with their families and friends."

"And mates?" he asked hopefully.

I smiled and ran my fingers through his soft hair. "And mates. The bond between a shifter and their mate is everlasting and unbreakable. Once a shifter has found his or her mate, they dedicate their lives to caring for, providing for, and protecting that person. They can never be without them, and they can never love or desire another. They will move heaven and earth to make sure that person is happy. They will reject anyone who disrespects their mate, or kill anyone who tries to bring them harm. But most importantly, they will love them without limits for the rest of time."

"Wow," Rory whispered. He licked his dry lips and asked, "And that's how you feel about me?"

"Always," I answered seriously. "I told you that I recognized you by scent and instinct. Since the moment I came in contact with you, my body has called out for you. I long for your presence and your touch. A desperate need burns inside of me to look after you and make you happy. I fell in love the moment I laid eyes on you, and once I spoke to you and got to know you, I fell even deeper. You are the other half of my heart and soul and I can't live without you."

"Is that why it hurts when I think about leaving your house or when I didn't kiss you?"

"Yes. Even though you are human, Fate has perfectly matched us and your body can feel the pull between us. We need each other to both survive and thrive. Once we are bonded, we will be linked together for all time and nothing can separate us."

"How do we bond? Is meeting and falling in love not enough? Is bonding like a marriage?"

"In a sense," I replied, bobbing my head back and forth. "But it is much deeper and stronger than any marriage or human union. It links our very souls and lives together. You will inherit my increased metabolism to keep your body strong and vibrant, as well as speed up your healing processes if you become injured. You will also be granted with immortality. We will live on this earth together and I promise to fill every day with love and happiness."

"I'll live forever?" Rory looked shocked as he shook his head in disbelief. "Will I just keep getting older? Will I get all wrinkly and saggy with brittle bones and illnesses? Because that doesn't seem like a great way to live, if I'm honest."

"I love your honesty." I appreciated that I never had to guess what he was thinking, and that he told me how he felt whether it was what I wanted to hear or not. That characteristic would make him a wonderful leader. I pecked his lips and gave him a wide smile. "But you don't need to worry about that. The aging process of shifters and their mates slow around the natural age of thirty to forty. We are also immune to all diseases."

"How old are you?" he asked, tipping his head to the side.

"Seventy three."

"Damn, you look great for your age."

I laughed out loud at my mate's frankness and appreciation. "Thank you. I'm glad you approve."

"Especially since you'll look like that forever," he nodded, and I chuckled again. "But what about me? I've got at least ten years of aging to do; I'm sure my appearance will change. What if you don't like the changes?"

"It's impossible. You will only grow more handsome and desirable in my eyes."

"Okay, good answer." My grin widened at his humor and sweetness. "So, is the bonding like a ceremony or something?"

Oh, right. I still haven't answered that question. "Not exactly. We can have a ceremony if you like; I will do anything you wish to make you happy, but to complete our bond, I must spill my seed inside you and give you my mating bite."

"Oh." Rory blinked wide eyes. "Screw a wedding; that sounds *way* more fun."

I laughed at his reaction, but also wanted to make sure he understood the gravity of our bond. "Once we are mated, nothing will be able to separate us; not even death. We will be immortal by natural causes, but *can* be killed. If one of our lives is cut short, the other's death will immediately follow so that we never have to live apart."

Rory let out a long breath. "I understand. I'll be careful to not put myself in harm's way so that I won't risk your eternal life. And I know that you'll protect me the best you can."

"I promise." I sealed my vow with a kiss to his forehead. "Once we are bonded, time apart beyond a few hours will cause us physical pain. I ask that you live here with me. If you wish to continue working, I will respect that and gladly take you to and from your job and watch over you while you work. If you'd rather quit your job, I will provide you with everything you need and you can spend your days doing the things that make you happy."

"So if I wanted to quit and just spend my time hiking and taking photographs and watching movies with you or just loving you all day in our bed, you wouldn't think I was a giant lazy lump?"

"Not a chance." Honestly, I couldn't think of anything I'd love more than providing for my mate and allowing him to only do activities he enjoyed, but I didn't want to sway Rory's decision in any way.

Rory tapped his fingers on his chin as he thought. "So you're telling me that I will live forever with my drop dead sexy wolf husband in the house that he built, where he will protect me, provide for me, and love me for the rest of time?"

"Yes." I scrunched up my eyebrows as Rory tucked his arms inside the sleeves of his shirt. "What are you doing?"

"I'm getting naked," he replied like it should be obvious. "So that we can get to the bonding."

A growl of lust and anticipation rumbled in my chest. Rory stopped taking his shirt off, letting it hang around his neck like a scarf, and looked at me with rounded eyes. "I'm sorry, I didn't mean to scare you. I'm just excited."

"You didn't scare me," he responded with a slow shake of his head. "You're so turned on that you went all primal for me; that's hot as hell." He reached out and unbuttoned my shirt as my breaths grew quicker. Rory leaned over and pressed the side of his face to my bare chest. "Can you do it again?" I let out a deep, slow growl and smiled as a shiver rocked through my mate's body. "Good lord, I think I could get off just by you lying on top of me and doing that."

"I *really* want to test your theory," I admitted. "And we will; we have all the time in the world to discover together everything that drives you wild and gives you pleasure, but for now, I need you Rory. I need to take you and claim you as mine. Knowing that you accept me and want me is setting my blood alight with desire."

"I feel it too." Rory nuzzled his cheek against my chest. "My pulse is racing and my hands are shaky. I feel like I might go crazy if you don't take me."

That was all I needed to hear. I pulled Rory into my arms and stood in one fluid motion. I carried him into our bedroom as he pecked gentle kisses up my neck, only fanning the flames burgeoning inside me. I laid my mate on top of the comforter and popped his shirt over his head before tossing it to the floor. I shrugged my own top off of my shoulders as Rory kicked off his sneakers and socks.

I couldn't take my eyes off of him as I stepped out of my boots and socks and unbuttoned my jeans. Rory's hands trembled and faltered as he pawed at his own pants. Once I lowered my bottoms and boxers to the floor, I gripped Rory's jeans by the ankles and in one swift yank, pulled them free of his lithe body. He gasped and stared at me with a fiery, passionate gaze. My lover liked it when I showed my strength and desire.

I peeled his briefs down his legs and was once again struck by the beauty and suppleness of his body. It was a sight I'd never get tired of admiring. I tossed his underwear to the floorboards and opened the drawer of the nightstand. I retrieved a fresh bottle of lube, provided by Rowan's visit to town. I ripped the plastic wrapper open with my teeth and spit it into the floor before tossing the bottle onto the bed.

"Have I mentioned it's super hot when you get wild?" Rory asked with fire in his eyes. His hand trailed down his body and gripped the base of his hard cock. He moaned as he gave himself a slow stroke.

I grabbed both of his wrists, peeling his hand off of his shaft. I pinned both of his arms above his head and climbed onto the bed, straddling his legs between my thighs. I lowered my face until it was only an inch from his. "*I* give you pleasure. *I* touch your pretty cock. *I* work this beautiful little body into a frenzy until you call out *my* name and come for *me*." What can I say? Shifters are territorial bastards; especially alphas. Even the sight of Rory's own hand on his dick made me envious.

Rory's eyes slid closed and he swallowed hard. "Sweet jesus, I almost came already." Knowing my words alone got him so worked up made my cock throb and leak.

"Not yet, sweetheart. Not until I'm inside your perfect little ass." Rory's nostrils flared as he took a deep breath. "Keep these here," I instructed, squeezing his wrists gently. My mate's eyes popped open and he quickly nodded his agreement.

I sat up on my knees and brought Rory's legs to the outside of mine. I eased each of his feet up and planted them on the mattress so his knees were bent and I had an uninhibited view of his little pink pucker.

"Look at you," I whispered as I trailed my hands up his thighs. "My god, you're gorgeous." I wedged my fingers beneath his ass and squeezed his soft flesh in my large palms. Each of his sweet little ass cheeks fit perfectly into my hands. I ran my thumb up his crack and brushed it across his hole, making his entire body shake. "You like that?" Rory nodded so hard the mattress squeaked. "You just wait; I'm gonna make you feel incredible."

I pressed my thumb more firmly against Rory's pucker and circled his sensitive flesh. "You don't know how happy it makes me that I'm the first man to touch you here." I would never hold having any past lovers against my mate, but I can't deny the thrill and pride it gave me to be his first. "I'll be the first and only man to ever touch you. This sweet little ass is mine forever; *you're* mine forever."

"Forever," Rory repeated in a breathy whisper. "Please, Phoenix, I can't wait any longer." As he spoke, I was entranced by a glistening drop of pre-cum that beaded on his tip and slowly dripped down his length. I licked my lips but pulled my gaze away to retrieve the bottle of lube. My lover shivered with anticipation as I clicked the cap open and poured some of the slick liquid onto my hand.

I touched my wet finger to Rory's hole and pushed until just the tip popped inside. My mate moaned long and loud as I slowly inched my slick digit into his hot channel. "You're so tight," I grunted through clenched teeth. It was hard to reign in my arousal when I was picturing how amazing his tight little asshole was going to feel wrapped around my cock.

Rory answered with only panted breaths. My lover was too worked up to speak. "It's okay," I soothed. "I'm gonna get you all loosened up for me. I'll take good care of you, sweetheart." It was not only my duty as his mate, but my greatest pleasure.

As I pulsed my finger back and forth, Rory's muscles thinned and loosened, allowing me to glide easier within him. "Good job, sweetheart," I crooned. "Just keep breathing nice and deep. I'm gonna add another one." I touched a second fingertip to his rosebud and slid it in beside the first. Rory hissed at the stretch. "Are you okay?"

"Yeah," he answered with a grunt. "It just burns a little."

I stilled my hand to allow Rory time to adjust to the intrusion. He kept his breathing slow and deep, but there was still a trace of discomfort on his face. I knew how to distract him from any pain he was feeling. I lowered my head and touched my tongue to the base of his dick. I licked up the side of his heated flesh, collecting the salty drop that captured my attention earlier.

"Oh god," Rory moaned. His head tipped back in pleasure and his ring of muscle loosened around my fingers. I swirled my tongue around his tip, licking up every drip that leaked out of him. When I dipped the tip of my tongue into his slit, Rory cried out and bared down, sinking my fingers all the way inside of him.

Moving quickly to keep him focused on the pleasure instead of the pain, I parted my lips and took his length into my mouth. I swallowed him down to the root, nestling my lips against his coarse cropped hair.

"Oh Phoenix," Rory groaned, gripping the pillow above his head, "That feels incredible, baby." I slowly pulled my lips up until they were circled around his crown before slamming back down, burying him again in the heat of my throat. "Fuck yes! More! *Please*!" My mate's naughty pleas spurred me on. I bobbed my head up and down, sucking his dick so hard my cheeks hollowed. I took every inch of him until his tip brushed against the back of my throat and swallowed around him, milking his flesh and drinking the steady stream of pre-cum that poured out of him.

All the while, I worked my fingers in and out of his ass. Rory seemed to no longer feel any discomfort as I spread my digits apart and circled them around, stretching and preparing his channel. I rotated my wrist and curled my fingers up to rub along a soft patch of flesh on the top of his passage.

Rory cried out and slammed his arms down to grip the sheets at his side before quickly pinning them back over his head.

My mate was so intent on pleasing me and doing what I asked of him and it made my heart swell. I showed my appreciation by deep throating his cock once more as I rubbed the pads of my fingers in tight circles against his prostate. Rory's whole body trembled and his hips bucked off of the mattress, burying his dick even further down my throat.

"Please, Phoenix; I'm so close, but I don't want to come yet. I want to feel your big dick inside me. Take me, baby."

I pulled my fingers free of his ass and dropped his dick from my mouth as a hungry growl ripped out of me. Rory shivered again as he moaned and spread his legs further apart. I poured a generous glob of lube over the length of my cock and pressed my tip to his prepared hole.

"Deep breath and push out," I instructed. Rory nodded and breathed in deeply. As I pressed the head of my dick to his opening, Rory pushed out against me. My crown popped through his ring and we both moaned aloud as I slowly sank every inch of my thick cock inside him. "Is that okay?" I asked when my pubes were nestled against his balls. As much as I wanted to give my mate the ride of his life, I needed to take my time with him and ensure his comfort.

"It's good," he panted. "Please move."

He didn't have to tell me twice. I slowly pulled back until just my fat tip was inside him and steadily pushed back in. "You're doing so good," I crooned. "So good for me, sweetheart."

"And it feels good?" he asked with a look of desperate longing on his face.

"It feels incredible." I pulled back again and slid into him a little quicker. "Oh, Rory, you're so tight and hot for me." I picked up my pace, pulsing my hips back and forth in a steady rhythm. His passage sucked against me and pulled me deeper inside with every push. "Oh god, I've never felt anything like this." I moaned as I watched Rory's little asshole stretch and gobble up every inch of my length. "So fucking sexy."

I gripped my mate's ankles and wrapped his legs around my hips. "Just like that," I told him and he nodded again, locking his ankles behind my back. I circled my hands around his slim hips and pulled his body down onto me as I rocked up into him.

"Fuck!" Rory's cry made me pause and I looked at him with wide eyes, worried I hurt him. "Please don't stop. It feels so good. You're hitting a spot that-" He screamed again when I snapped my hips back and slammed into him. "There!"

"That's your sweet spot," I growled as I moved even quicker, pistoning my hips back and forth while rubbing the special place inside him that had my sweet mate falling apart. Rory moaned and thrashed, squeezing the pillow behind his head until his fingers turned white. He used his legs to pull me even deeper into him as he cursed at the ceiling.

Rory chanted, "So good," over and over as I slammed my body into him, pounding his tight little asshole with everything I had. Sweat poured down both of our faces and my mate's chest heaved with ragged breaths. "I'm close!" he yelled, looking at me pleadingly.

I wanted to give Rory everything he needed. I let loose of one of his hips and wrapped my fist around his red, leaking cock. I jacked him furiously, pumping my wrist in time with my hips as they crashed into him. My mate's back bowed off of the mattress, any pain in his side long forgotten due to the ecstasy coursing through him. His dick swelled in my hand and he screamed my name as he exploded.

Thick white cords spurted against Rory's stomach as he moaned and trembled beneath me. His eyes rolled back in his head and his ass clenched around me as he lost himself to his release. My balls lifted toward my body and pressure bloomed in my pelvis. I gripped his hips once again and slammed him down onto me, burying my dick as deep inside of him as possible. I growled out my lover's name as I erupted.

My hot seed pumped into him, painting his internal walls and my heart leapt. *It's time.* Rory's eyes slowly opened and focused on me, gazing at me with love and wonder. He knew what was coming. He gave me a gentle smile and nod, and I pounced.

Rory whimpered as I pulled my spent dick from his hole. I leaned my body over him and allowed my fangs to elongate to their full length. I clasped them around the flesh where his neck met his shoulder and bit down until my teeth scraped against his collar bone. Rory screamed and his dick jerked against me as another hot burst shot between our stomachs.

I retracted my fangs and smiled as I watched the wound close and morph into a dark pink scar. Now that we were bonded together, Rory's skin healed quickly into the beautiful mark he'd wear forever. I tore my gaze from the incredible sight to look into my mate's eyes and was taken aback by the way they shimmered as he stared back at me.

"We're linked together now, aren't we?" he asked in a whisper, as if out of respect for the moment.

"Forever," I whispered back. "I love you so much, Rory."

"I love you too, Phoenix."

I took his lips in a slow, tender kiss, pouring my care and affection into him, and hummed happily when I pulled away. I loved him so much it was literally warming my heart. Actually, my entire chest was overtaken by a tingling, pleasant heat. I looked down and my eyes filled with unshed tears. "Look, sweetheart."

Rory followed my gaze and gasped at the faint light emanating from my tattoo. The light arced from my chest to his, casting his smooth, fair skin in a soft glow. My mate watched in wide-eyed, stunned silence as a thick black line appeared on his flesh. The line broke apart, swirling and dancing across Rory's skin as it etched the same howling wolf pattern that marked my body onto his. Once the design was complete, the light that connected us slowly faded away.

I swallowed hard and looked into Rory's eyes, finding they were swimming with moisture just as mine were. My feelings of wonder, love and gratitude reflected back at me in their glistening depths.

"You are now a member of the Pine Ridge Pack," I told him, trying my best to keep my voice even. "Stone and Rowan are your brothers. They are honor bound to protect you, their Alpha's mate. You will help me to lead and guide them, along with any future members of our pack. You and I are eternally bonded as fated mates; nothing but death can break our bond. You are my greatest treasure. I vow to always protect you, provide for you, support you and love you with everything I am."

A tear slipped beneath Rory's glasses and down his cheek. I gently wiped it away as he blew out a shaky breath. "You've opened my eyes to a world I never knew existed; not only the world of Fate and shifters, but one where I'm accepted and loved for who I am. I'm not big or strong like the others in the pack, but I'm loyal and honest. I'll be there for my brothers the best way that I can and help them in any way they need. And I'll always be true to you and love you with all my heart for the rest of time."

Rory's beautiful words warmed my insides. His promises mended my soul and for the first time in my life, I felt complete. I laid my forehead against his and closed my eyes, giving myself over to the peace and happiness that filled me. I inhaled his sweet breaths into my lungs, taking every part of him I could into myself. We were one, now and always.

I don't know how long I held him, listening to the gentle pattern of his breathing and feeling the soft beat of his heart against my chest. Time didn't matter; we had so much of it together. Rory's previous human lifeline was now a mere blink in his existence. I thanked Fate and the universe for allowing me to spend eternity with someone so perfect.

"Phoenix?" Rory asked in a gentle voice. I raised my head and gazed upon him, longing for whatever wonderful thoughts he wanted to share with me in this precious time. "My cum is getting cold and sticky on my stomach."

I blinked in surprise before bursting into laughter. Rory was honest, funny, and always unpredictable in the best way. "I'm truly blessed," I thought out loud, making my mate's face screw up in confusion as I chuckled some more. "Come on, sweetheart, let's get you cleaned up."

I climbed from the bed and offered Rory a hand. When he stood beside me, he shifted his legs around as his head cocked to the side. "That feels kinda good. I'm a little sore and stretched, but it's nice." He smiled at me for a moment before his eyes popped open wide. "Oh god, you're leaking out of me!" Rory hurried to the bathroom in a wide-legged waddle, sending me into another fit of laughter. I folded my hands on my stomach as I laughed out loud, replaying my mate's panicked shuffle over and over in my mind.

"You are too precious," I told him when I finally got myself under control and made my own way into the bathroom. I stopped in my tracks when I found Rory standing before the mirror, admiring his new tattoo in the reflection. He gingerly traced a finger over the tribal design with a pretty smile playing on his lips. My mate could flip the mood from silly and playful to sweet and reverent in the blink of an eye. He was amazing.

"What do you think?" I asked as I stepped behind him, leaning down to rest my chin on his shoulder.

"I love it. It's beautiful, but it's so much more; it links me to you and the rest of our pack." My heart leapt at the way Rory so easily referred to the pack as 'ours'. "It's like I finally have a family who wants me and will be there for me forever."

"You *do* have a family, sweetheart. Like I told you, Stone and Rowan are you brothers and I'm-"

"My wolf husband," Rory finished, and I chuckled again. He'd used the term before and I liked it. It showed he accepted me in every form, and I knew the gravity the word 'husband' held in human terms. "I guess it's not just me and Dax anymore." As soon as the words left his lips, Rory's body deflated and sadness swam in his eyes.

"What's wrong?" I wrapped my arms around his waist, giving him support.

"I was so excited about our bonding and our pack, I didn't think about Dax. I'll have to say goodbye to him. He'll grow older without me and I'll lose him. I'll live forever with just the memory of my best friend."

My heart broke for him. I had my best friends by my side my whole life and always would. I tightened my grip on him and kissed his cheek. "I'm so sorry, Rory. But because Dax is important to you, he's important to me and the rest of the pack. We will take care of him and look after him to ensure his happiness and well-being. And you have many more decades with him, sweetheart."

Rory wiped his eyes and gave me a little smile. "You're right. I've still got so much time with him and I want to enjoy every second." He turned his head to kiss my lips and sighed. "I'm sorry I brought down the mood."

"Don't be. I want to hear your worries and all of your thoughts. I'm here for you and will help any way I can, even if it's just to listen. That's what wolf husbands do."

Rory huffed a laugh and gave me another kiss. "Thank you."

"It's my pleasure." I released him and stepped towards the shower. "I'll start our water. I'm going to wash your beautiful little body and then rub your shoulders and back until all of your worries are long gone."

"That sounds incredible." I bent down and twisted the knobs, adjusting the temperature of our shower when Rory's gasp made me stand up quickly and spin to face him. "Look at this!" He pointed to his side in the reflection of the mirror.

I stepped closer and hurriedly looked him over. "What's wrong? I don't see anything."

"Exactly! My bruises are gone." Rory poked a finger into his side. "And my ribs don't hurt anymore."

A smile stretched across my face. "Your body is healed because of our bonding. You have my increased metabolism and healing now, remember?"

Rory nodded. "That must be why I'm craving a big, juicy steak."

I laughed as I shook my head at my silly mate. "Well then, I guess I'll have to wash you, massage you and then cook you a delicious dinner of steak and potatoes."

Rory gave my lips a fierce, quick kiss. "Have I mentioned I love you?"

My heart nearly swelled too big for my chest. "Sweetheart, I hope you never stop telling me." And I hoped he never got tired of hearing it in return.

Chapter Ten

Rory

Life is amazing. For the past couple of weeks since Phoenix's and my bonding, I'd been spending a lot of time with Stone and Rowan. They welcomed me with open arms into the pack and vowed their loyalty and protection to me. I promised my loyalty, honesty and guidance in return, and Phoenix looked so proud I thought he might pop.

Rowan was excited when I asked him for lessons about nature and healing. He took me on a long hike (while I wore the new hiking boots Phoenix bought me, I might add) each day, pointing out different plants and explaining their medicinal qualities as I jotted down notes in a beautiful leather journal Phoenix gave me. My husband (okay, maybe not *technically*, but he never corrected me when I called him that, so I ran with it) joined us on our walks because he couldn't handle being away from me for so long, but he kept to the background and let Rowan take the lead. He only interrupted to offer me water and to make sure I wasn't getting too tired. Surprisingly, my endurance and strength grew every day.

Rowan and I also had several lengthy discussions about mates and human customs and relationships. The man craved companionship and love and I hoped he found his fated match soon. He was one of the sweetest men I'd ever met in my life, and he deserved happiness.

My interactions with Stone were much different. At first, he didn't say much when we hung out. I never thought he was being rude or standoffish; he just wasn't a man of many words. He and I watched a couple of action movies together and I enjoyed sharing space with him and reacting to the films together, but I wanted more. I asked Phoenix what Stone liked and found out he was a bit of a weapons expert and a keen survivalist.

When I asked Stone to give me some pointers in self-defense and weapons training, he came alive. It was like he became a different person; open, talkative and surprisingly, a wonderful teacher. He spent hours every day showing me how to tie knots and set traps. He joined Rowan, Phoenix and me on our hikes and while Rowan showed me medicinal plants, Stone pointed out berries and flowers that could be used as food and which ones to avoid.

Self-defense training was...interesting. The first time Stone tried to show me how to fight, I missed a block and got a slap to the side of the head. Phoenix became enraged at Stone for harming me (even though I tried to tell him it didn't hurt) and tackled him to the ground. They wrestled in the dirt, fists and curses flying as I screamed at them to stop. It wasn't until Rowan retrieved a pitcher of cold water from his cabin and tossed it on them that they separated. They made up immediately and laughed the whole thing off as I stared at them and decided shifters were the strangest, most intense people I'd ever met.

From then on, my training consisted of me punching a dummy Stone made out of some wood planks and sand bags. Stone also showed me how to safely handle a knife and the best way to strike with one. He even gave me an awesome tactical knife that I now wore on my hip in a holster every day.

I talked to Dax on the phone daily, but hadn't seen him because of his crazy work hours between both of his jobs. We had plans to meet up the following weekend and I was excited to introduce him to Phoenix. Dax was surprised but excited when I told him I'd quit my job at the grocery store and moved in with Phoenix. He said he was happy for me and would support me in everything I did. He was the best friend I could imagine.

Perhaps my favorite new development was the pack dinners we now had three times a week. Each household took turns preparing and hosting dinner for the others. When I suggested them as a way to relax and bond together, Phoenix showered me with praise, saying I was the glue that held the pack together and that he couldn't be prouder of me. Rowan echoed his compliments and was excited for the delicious food and male bonding the meals brought. Stone just shrugged his agreement, saying he'd gladly let someone else cook for him twice a week.

But now as Stone rose from our kitchen table rubbing his stomach with a smile on his face, it was obvious he loved the dinners.

"Thank god for shifter metabolism," Stone groaned as he shuffled toward the living room. "What was in that pie Rory; blackberries? It was delicious."

"Oh, I made it with those little berries you showed me in the woods. What were they called...Pokeweed?"

Stone's eyes were huge as he rounded on me. "You fed us Pokeweed? Holy shit, you've just poisoned us all! Dammit, Rory, I told you *not* to eat those! You're gonna get yourself killed! I-"

He stopped ranting when I burst into laughter. "The pie *was* blackberry. Phoenix had some in his freezer. Sorry, I couldn't help myself." Phoenix and Rowan joined in on my laughter as Stone squinted his eyes at me. Finally, the big lug's lips curled into a smirk.

"Okay, okay, you got me." He gave me a playful shove on the shoulder. "You're alright, Roar."

"I knew you loved me," I teased, batting my eyelashes. A growl rumbled in Phoenix's chest as he stared daggers at his friend. I cooled my husband down with a kiss to his cheek while Stone just rolled his eyes at us and snorted a laugh as he went back into the living room.

"Ah, I've been eyeing this chair all night," he said as he sat in Phoenix's favorite recliner and squished his butt around. Phoenix glared at Stone again.

"You wouldn't be sitting in that chair if you knew what we did in it last night," I shrugged and Stone's eyes snapped to me. "We turned up the massage so it'd vibrate Phoenix's balls while I rode him." Phoenix and I had done nothing of the sort, but I couldn't help teasing Stone.

"God dammit, you've ruined this chair for me forever!" Stone yelled as he jumped out of it.

"Thank you," Phoenix whispered in my ear.

"You can thank me by actually making that scene happen later," I whispered back. Phoenix growled low and nipped my earlobe.

"Is the couch clean?" Stone asked, pointing to a sofa cushion. I scrunched up my face and held my hand out, rotating it back and forth in a 'so-so' motion. "I'm sitting on the floor," he grumped, crossing his arms over his chest and slamming his big ass on the ground.

Rowan laughed and patted my back. "How did I ever make it without you here to help me irritate him?" He walked over to the couch and settled in comfortably as Stone shook his head at him.

Just then, a noise pierced the air beyond our cabin's walls. It was faint to my human ears, but Rowan, Stone and Phoenix all flinched at the sound. Stone jumped up from the floor and Rowan was also on his feet in a blink.

"What was that?" I asked, looking quickly between the three men. I didn't like the looks of concern on their faces.

Phoenix didn't answer as he crossed the room and opened the front door. A few moments later, the same sound splintered through the quiet evening air. "Gunshots."

Cracks and pops filled the living room, and I looked to the sound to find Rowan and Stone in their wolf forms, stepping free of tattered clothing. I'd seen both of their wolves many times over the past couple of weeks, but I'd never witnessed them as they were now; with their teeth bared and the hair on their shoulders standing up.

The two of them bolted from our cabin and Phoenix cupped my cheeks in his hands and looked at me seriously. "I have to go with them. I have to protect the pack from whatever's out there, and protect the lands."

I hated that he had to go out into a potentially dangerous situation, but I understood. It was his duty as Alpha to keep the pack safe and help anyone else who may be in danger. "Be careful."

Phoenix gave me a quick, firm kiss. "I will. Lock the door and don't answer it until you see us return." With that, he dropped his hands from my face and shifted into his powerful wolf form. He sprinted out of the door and into the forest after his friends.

I scooted his boots and ripped clothing away from the door so that I could latch it shut. I locked the handle and the deadbolt before stepping back from the entryway and sitting on the sofa. I took my knife from its holster and gripped the handle tightly. Hopefully I was overreacting and the situation would be settled quickly, but I felt safer having protection in my hand.

Minutes ticked by and I breathed a sigh of relief when I heard multiple growls coming from outside. *They're back.* I leapt from the couch and jogged to the window. When I looked outside, my body instantly grew cold with fear. There were several wolves outside the house, but I didn't recognize any of them. They weren't my pack.

I quickly counted eleven wolves, all of whom were snarling, growling and snapping their teeth as they gathered onto the porch.

I stepped away from the window and plastered my back against the front door. *Remember what Rowan told you on your hikes; wolves aren't indigenous to this region. These aren't animals; they're shifters.*

Oddly enough, that didn't make me feel any better. Plus, it was hard to believe; when I looked at the wolves on my porch, I didn't see any traces of humor or humanity behind their cold eyes. They looked feral and wicked, like they couldn't wait for the chance to tear me apart.

I swallowed hard as I heard the telltale sound of one of the wolves on the other side of the door shifting forms. "We know you're in there," a man's deep voice taunted. "We just want to talk." I wasn't dumb enough to believe that. The doorknob jiggled as the man tried to turn it. "You don't want my men coming in after you." I clutched my knife tightly in my hand. If they *did* manage to get in, I wasn't going to go down without a fight. "Last chance," the man warned. The air crackled with the sound of many shifts happening at once. "Take him."

I jumped when a fist crashed through the window to my right. Many hands gripped and pulled shards of glass away, widening the hole. They healed quickly from the dozens of cuts that appeared as the sharp edges tore their skin. Realizing they'd be inside very soon, I ran into the bedroom and locked its door behind me. I made it to the window and got it open just as footsteps stomped through the living room. I climbed outside and ran as soon as my feet hit the grass.

I sprinted as fast as I could toward the treeline where Phoenix, Stone and Rowan disappeared. I hoped I could lose the other shifters in the dense woods and that once I'd put enough distance between us, I could call out to my pack for help. But before I made it out of the clearing where our homes sat, I heard steady footfalls behind me. I turned around just in time to see a man shift into a huge brown wolf.

I knew as I watched him speed towards me that I had no chance of outrunning him. I hid the blade of my knife along my wrist and knelt down on one knee. The wolf didn't slow down even though I wasn't in a threatening stance. There was no question he meant me harm. Once he was within several feet of me, he leapt at me with his teeth bared.

I flipped the blade of my knife around and gripped the handle. As the wolf descended on me, I plunged my weapon into its chest. It let out a pained whine as its body weight knocked me onto my back. It was still and quiet on top of me. I managed to wriggle out from under it and stood up. My breath caught as I looked upon its lifeless body; I'd never harmed anything beyond the sandbag dummy Stone made. But I didn't have a choice. It was him or me, and I wasn't about to give up the life I shared with Phoenix, let alone cut his short.

The sight of a group of men running towards me ripped me from my thoughts. I knelt down again and pulled my blade from the wolf's body, shuddering when its blood trickled down my fingers. I'd lucked out with this one wolf, but there was no way I could take on the group of huge, angry men on my own. I needed help; I needed my pack.

I tipped my head back to the sky and cupped my hands around my mouth. I gave my best howl, hoping it carried on the evening breeze better than a human yell, and knowing Phoenix would recognize my voice. Just as the crowd was closing in on me, I heard the echo of three distinct howls. My pack was on its way.

*****

Phoenix

I sped from the cabin and followed my friends into the woods. I quickly caught up with them and leapt to the head of the pack. Rowan flanked my right side and Stone covered my left as we ran toward the area from where we heard the gunshots.

My first thought was that someone was illegally hunting on state land. If that was the case, we needed to be careful; three wolves would be the perfect target for a hunter. If the person was still out walking around, our best course of action would be to shift out of sight and yell to scare them away. One or all of us could follow them at a distance to their car and get the information from their tags to turn over to the authorities.

The other option was that we weren't dealing with a hunter, but someone up to much darker activities. It was possible someone was injured in the woods, or worse. We needed to be alert and ready for anything.

I sniffed the air as we ran, following the faint trail of gunpowder. As we went deeper into the woods, a second scent mixed in. It was unpleasant but familiar. I searched my brain for the smell and stopped in my tracks when I placed it. Rowan and Stone paused behind me. I shifted into human form and my friends followed.

"What's wrong?" Stone asked, surveying our surroundings.

"Do you smell that?"

Rowan sniffed the air and flinched. "Shifters."

"*Wolf* shifters," I corrected. "It's Raven and his men." Though the scent was one I hadn't encountered in decades, I'd never forget the acrid stench of my brother. But why were they here? We weren't anywhere near their pack lands. And why were they shooting? Realization dawned on me and my stomach churned. Raven had lured me away from my home and my mate with the sound. "It's a trap."

Rowan gasped. "Rory!"

The three of us shifted and sprinted back toward our cabins. I pushed myself harder than ever before, desperate to get to my mate. Dirt flung in every direction as my paws tore up the earth. We were nearly to the treeline when a distraught howl pierced the air. It was Rory calling out for help. I yowled my reply at the same time as Rowan and Stone. We were close; I needed my sweet mate to hold on.

We burst into the clearing and my eyes darted over the scene before me, trying to take in every detail at once. Rory gripped the knife Stone gave him in his shaking hand. The blade was covered in blood and at my mate's feet was the lifeless body of a wolf. Pride and guilt warred in my chest; Rory was so strong and courageous to defend himself, but I wished I'd never left him alone.

Ten men were closing in on Rory with hatred in their eyes. Raven was at the front of the pack. My brave mate dropped into a defensive stance, ready to fight. But he wouldn't be fighting alone any more. I stepped in front of Rory and my friends stood at his sides. My mate let out a relieved sigh and ran his hand down my back.

We shifted and Rory's arms wrapped around my waist from behind. "They showed up right after you left," he explained quickly. "They burst into the house. I got away, but they came after me. I don't even know who they are or what they want. I had to kill one, Phoenix. I didn't want to. I tried showing I wasn't a threat, but he attacked me. I had to! I-"

"You did great," Stone interrupted. Rory jerked against me as my friend slapped his back in approval. I could only imagine the pride Stone felt at Rory's use of the training he gave to him.

"I'm so proud of you, sweetheart," I said without taking my eyes off of my brother, who was mere feet away. "You are brave and strong. I'm sorry we left you, but we're here now. Everything will be okay." Rory nodded against my spine and tightened his grip on me.

"Ah, there you are," Raven said as he and his pack stopped advancing. Long, scraggly black hair cascaded over his shoulders and face. Eyes the color of my own shone against his pale, sharp features. "I was wondering when you'd show up."

"If you wanted me, why draw me out into the woods?"

"I heard rumors that you lived around these parts, and convinced some local hikers to keep an eye on you." I had no doubt his 'convincing' consisted of threats and force. "They reported back to me that you were spending a lot of time on the trails with three men. I knew you had such a meager pack of two, and was able to piece together that you'd met your mate. And I needed leverage," he shrugged. "You have a tendency to run, but I knew that if I had your mate, you'd do anything to protect him. I wasn't expecting him to be such a fighter, though." His lips twisted into an evil grin. "I suppose opposites attract." The group of men behind him laughed and smirked at me.

"I hate you for what you did to our parents, but you're still my brother. I left because I didn't want to fight you, Raven. I hoped in time you'd mature and become the leader the pack needed. I didn't want father's death to be in vain."

"Those are a coward's excuses," Raven spat.

"You *dare* call our Alpha a coward?" Stone growled, stepping up to my left side.

"Alpha Phoenix is strong and valiant," Rowan added, flanking my right. "Traits you know nothing about."

"I know nothing of strength? I struck down a powerful Alpha!" Raven argued. "I took control of his pack. I am the fiercest leader in these lands; proven by the way weak members have moved on, unable to live up to my high standards." Cockiness and greed had brought him here. He wasn't happy with what he had; he wanted everything. Especially if that meant taking it from me, a man he believed to be weaker and less brave than him.

Rory surprised me by releasing my waist and nudging his way between me and Rowan, staring my brother down. "Instilling fear and making threats doesn't equal strength. Phoenix protects his pack and cares about our well-being. He supports us and encourages us to be our best. *That's* the strength of a leader." I rested my hand on Rory's shoulder and squeezed, silently thanking my mate for his words and boldness.

Raven's lip curled. "What do you know of strength? You're just a human, bred from weakness."

"A human who killed one of your men," Stone pointed out.

Raven merely shrugged. "An obviously expendable man if he got himself killed by a human." Sadly, I was unsurprised by the lack of empathy he had for the loss of a pack member, as well as the distaste he held for humans, whom he always believed to be a weaker species. "Besides, he disobeyed orders by attacking. I only wanted the human in my possession; I didn't want him killed. *You're* my prize." Another wicked smile crossed his face. "And I want to have the honor of collecting my trophy personally. Fight me."

"No," I answered firmly. "There's no reason for it. No more lives need to be lost tonight. Our packs have lived in peace for decades by staying away from each other. Our business is our own, as is yours. Leave here and take care of your pack."

The smirk vanished from his face. "You don't have a choice, brother." Raven's eyes grew cold and he held his head high to announce, "I challenge you to a fight to the death for control of your land, homes and pack." Raven's men cheered for their leader.

Vicious growls ripped from Rowan and Stone's throats. Rory gasped and stepped in front of me, staring pleadingly into my eyes. "Don't accept," he begged. "Give him the land and our houses. The four of us can move on together. We'll find somewhere else to live. All we need is each other. We know you're a great leader; you don't have to prove it this way. Don't give into his hatred."

Raven cackled a piercing laugh. "Stupid human; you don't know how any of this works." My pack mates growled louder, but they'd never attack without my permission.

I cupped Rory's cheeks in my hands and looked into his pretty chocolate eyes, which were glistening with fear and confusion. "If I don't accept his challenge, I surrender everything to him; not only our homes and land, but Stone, Rowan..." I swallowed hard before adding, "And you."

"Not really my type," Raven sneered, "But I have a feeling a few of my members would *love* to play with you." Those men agreed by cheering and shouting lewd comments at my mate. A tear slipped down Rory's cheek and I gently brushed it away with my thumb.

"It's the only way to keep you safe," I told him gently. His lip trembled as he gave a small nod.

"You have to win."

"I promise." I had no choice. If I lost, both my life and Rory's would end tonight, and Rowan and Stone would be forced to pledge their allegiance to Raven, or be killed as well. I kissed Rory soundly and hugged him tightly, reveling in the feel of his body against mine. I buried my nose into his hair and inhaled his sweet scent deeply into my lungs, praying it wasn't the last time. "I love you, Rory."

"I love you too," he replied in a shaky whisper.

I eased Rory next to Rowan, who tucked my mate under his arm. I stepped toe to toe with my brother and stared him in the eyes. "I accept your challenge."

Chapter Eleven

Rory

In mere minutes, the arena was set. In the clearing next to our homes, a wide circle was drawn in the dirt. Torches were placed around the ring, illuminating the area in firelight. As the stage was being prepared, Phoenix held me in his arms and whispered promises of loving me forever to try and calm me down. I was a wreck; when he and I bonded, I never envisioned something like this happening. Our very lives hung in the balance. I wasn't ready to say goodbye to the man who loved and cherished me, not to mention my pack family. My life was finally perfect, and it could all end tonight.

"It's time," Stone said sadly as he stepped next to Phoenix and me. I sobbed harder, burying my face into my husband's chest.

"It's okay," Phoenix whispered. He placed his finger under my chin and lifted until I looked up at him. "Be strong for me, Rory." He wiped my face dry and I managed to give him a slight nod. The last thing he needed was to be distracted by me. "I promise I won't fail you." He kissed my lips and stepped into the ring.

Stone took me under his arm and led me to the sideline. Rowan crowded next to my opposite side. My brothers were keeping watch over me and supporting me the best way they could. I looked around the ring to find Raven's pack spread out on the other side. All of the shifters were now dressed in a pair of sweatpants; it was a condition Phoenix put on the match for dignity and respect, and I was thankful for it.

"We can't enter the circle to help," Rowan explained to me, bending down to speak softly into my ear. "It would mean an automatic loss for Phoenix. No matter what happens, you must stay here with us." I swallowed hard and nodded my understanding.

"What will you do if Phoenix loses?" I asked quietly.

Rowan shook his head. "Don't think like that. He won't lose."

"Please," I begged. "I'll be gone. I need to know what will happen to you."

He gave me a sad smile. "I won't submit to Raven."

"Neither will I," Stone offered.

I knew from conversations I'd had with the pack about shifter culture that only alphas could challenge other alphas for leadership. Rowan and Stone were both betas, which meant they could either submit to Raven and accept him as their new alpha, or be executed. They'd already made up their minds.

"Promise me you won't go down without a fight," I pleaded, looking between them. "Take out as many as you can to avenge Phoenix."

"I promise," they both answered.

"And in case this is the last time I get to talk to you, I want you both to know how much it means to me to be in your pack. You've accepted me and taught me so much. I really do think of you as my brothers, and I love you both. If I have to die tonight, I'm glad it's with you by my side." I wished I could see Dax one last time, but I didn't want him here to witness this.

"It's been an honor and a privilege to have you as our Alpha's mate," Stone said, bowing his head.

"You are loyal and true," Rowan added, also while lowering his head. "We love you too, and we will always stand by your side." I gave them both the best smile I could muster before turning my attention to the ring.

Raven and Phoenix stood on opposite ends, staring one another down. They were of similar height and both had strong, muscular frames. They were well-matched, which didn't help to soothe my nerves.

One of Raven's men raised his hand and everyone fell quiet. "As the defending Alpha, Phoenix will now choose the form in which the match will be conducted."

All eyes fell to my husband, though his didn't budge from Raven. "I choose to fight in wolf form," Phoenix announced clearly.

Murmurs broke out amongst the crowd, but the man got everyone's attention once more. "Defender chooses wolf form. Remove your garments." Phoenix and Raven stepped out of their pants and tossed them out of the ring. It was a formality to show they weren't hiding any weapons, and to clear the stage of any obstructions. "Shift."

A moment later, the ring was filled by two large, powerful wolves. I knew Phoenix's brown wolf form well, and recognized Raven's pitch black wolf form as one of the malicious animals on my porch earlier.

"Begin!"

Both wolves dropped low to the ground and stalked around the circle. The hair on the scruff of their necks was standing upright, and their snouts were wrinkled, showing their teeth. Raven was the first to strike. He bounded toward Phoenix and sank his teeth into Phoenix's front leg.

Phoenix slammed his shoulder into his brother, knocking him to the ground. Raven dropped a mouthful of Phoenix's flesh and fur onto the grass. The wound stopped bleeding and closed within moments.

Phoenix charged toward his brother, but when he was within striking range, Raven dug his paw into the earth and flung dirt into Phoenix's eyes. He yelped and shook his head, trying to dislodge the debris.

"That slimy son of a bitch!" I yelled, furious at Raven's cheating. I took an instinctive step toward the circle, but Stone gripped me around the waist.

"We can't," he reminded me. "Raven is fighting dirty because he knows Phoenix is stronger."

While my poor mate was incapacitated, Raven charged at him and clamped his jaws around his throat. Phoenix blinked furiously, trying to clear his eyes as he attempted to yank free of the deadly hold, but Raven's teeth only sank deeper.

"No!" I clawed at Stone's arms, but his hold on me only tightened. "Let me go! Please, I can't watch him die!" I wrestled against him and kicked my legs, but I was no match for his strength. "I'll leave with Raven and his men, I don't care what they do to me. Please, just let me go to him!"

"I can't do that," Stone answered, his voice heavy with sadness.

"Phoenix would rather die than let you leave with Raven," Rowan added. He put his hand on my shoulder and squeezed. I had to do everything I could to keep that from happening.

"Fight!" I yelled to my husband. "Fight for me!" Phoenix stilled his jerky movements and looked at me. His eyes were now clear, but the light behind them was dimming. "You can't hold back. He's not your brother! *These* men are your brothers!" Stone's hold kept me from motioning toward him and Rowan. "They're your pack and they need you. *I* need you. You promised to protect me from anyone who tried to harm me." Tears once again streamed down my cheeks. "He's going to kill me too, Phoenix."

As soon as the words left my lips, something flickered in Phoenix's gaze. His eyes narrowed and intensified. He reared up on his back legs and dug his front claws into Raven's sides. Blood gushed from the gashes, painting the grass red beneath them. Raven loosened his hold and Phoenix managed to back away.

"Yes!" I cried. "*That's* my Alpha!" Stone whistled loudly over my head and Rowan clapped furiously.

Both wolves breathed heavily as their wounds closed. Once their bleeding stopped, they were right back at it. They rushed at each other and both of them lunged off of their powerful back legs. Their chests rammed together and they were a flurry of scratching claws, furious growls and snapping teeth.

A fire had been lit in Phoenix. Maybe he *had* been holding back because he still didn't want to fight his brother, but that was over. His love for me and his duty to his pack won out and urged him on. He was the picture of dominating intensity as he slashed Raven's flesh and bit chunks of skin and fur from his face and neck. My husband was a badass.

Phoenix threw all of his weight at Raven and knocked him to the ground. He was quick to wrap his jaws around his brother's neck and bite down. I heard bones crunch beneath his teeth and a gurgling sound coming from Raven's throat. Raven tried to kick Phoenix with his back legs, but he was too far away. Phoenix wasn't messing around any longer; he'd gone in for the kill. It looked like the fight would be over soon. But then all hell broke loose.

Four of Raven's men shifted into their wolf forms and leapt into the ring. The other five sprinted toward Stone, Rowan and me. It was too smooth and rehearsed to have been a spur of the moment move. I wondered if Raven had given them instructions to attack if the match took a negative turn.

Stone released me from his hold and met the attackers head on. A man with greasy brown hair took a swing at him, but Stone dodged it and slammed his fist into the man's face. His jaw unhinged and hung toward his chest. Before he even recovered from the shock, Stone wrapped his hands around the man's head and snapped his neck, dropping the limp body to the ground.

A blond man charged at Rowan, who easily flipped him over his shoulder. The man landed with a *thud* and before he could even stand up, Stone whistled to get Rowan's attention. He pulled a knife from a holster on his ankle and tossed it to Rowan, who flipped out the blade and plunged it into the man's chest. Yes, he was unarmed, but all rules were broken the moment Raven's men entered the circle.

I watched with wide eyes as Rowan and Stone each fought another man. Their moves were meticulous and their large bodies moved with more grace than I could fathom. I was so entranced by their fluid movements, I missed the last man approaching me from behind.

Thick, hairy arms wrapped around my chest and pinned my own arms to my sides. A whine left my lungs as the arms squeezed the air out of me. A *crack* sounded as a rib on my right side splintered. *I'm going to die. After all of the crazy shit of the night, I'm gonna die from some hairy asshole squeezing me to death.* I closed my eyes and centered myself. *No you're not. Stay strong for Phoenix and remember Stone's training.*

I opened my eyes and picked my left foot up from the ground. I dug the heel of my hiking boot into the man's shin and scraped down before stomping on his bare foot. The man grunted and loosened his hold. I took the opportunity to throw an elbow into his ribs and spin around to face him. I threw a hook at his jaw, but when my fist collided with his face, the only one who got hurt was me. A pain shot up from my knuckles into my wrist. I yelped and pulled my hand back as the man just smirked at me. Then all humor left his face as he popped his neck from side to side. *Oh shit.*

"Rory, duck!" sounded from behind me. I dropped to my knees before I could even place the voice. Something flew over my head and I looked up to see the handle of a knife protruding from the man's throat.

He staggered and fell backward, slamming into the ground as his eyes glassed over. I whipped around to see Stone smiling at me. "I saw your moves; nice work," he winked.

"Yeah, but the guy had a freaking concrete jaw," I whined, rubbing my knuckles. Stone chuckled as he helped me from the ground. "How many knives do you have, anyway?"

"On me? Only three more." *Only?*

"Are you okay?" Rowan asked as he jogged over to meet us, leaving a man on the ground whose head was facing the wrong way.

"Fine," I answered honestly. The pain in my hand and ribs were already ebbing away. *Thank god for the healing power I got from Phoenix.* "Shit, Phoenix!" I cried, pushing Rowan away. In all the commotion, I'd nearly forgotten about his own fight. I rushed to the ring, and Stone and Rowan were at my side immediately. I gasped and stopped in my tracks as I took in the scene.

Two wolf bodies were sprawled out on the ground with their throats ripped out. Apparently, at some point all of the other men had shifted into human forms, because a man with dark hair was nearly split down the middle with his entrails lying on the ground before him, and another red-haired man's neck was bent at an unnatural angle.

And then there was Raven. Or what was left of him. It looked like Phoenix finally released all of the anger and hatred he'd been holding onto all of these years, taking it all out on his brother, who truly deserved it. Raven's limbs were detached and his head was resting at least a foot away from his body. A look of pure terror was still etched onto his face. My man had single-handedly killed the five men who attacked him, all in a spectacular fashion. *No wonder he's the fucking alpha.*

Phoenix rose from the ground, where he was resting on his knees catching his breath. He was still naked from his shift and covered sporadically from head to toe in dried blood. He looked intense, commanding, powerful...like a leader I'd follow anywhere.

When he approached us, Rowan and Stone stepped forward and tipped their heads to the side, baring their throats to Phoenix. They were submitting themselves to his leadership again. Phoenix raised his left hand, holding up his index and middle fingers. He tapped his fingers to the side of Stone's throat, acknowledging his submission and promising his protection.

"Thank you, Alpha," Stone said with a slight bow and stepped backward.

Phoenix then tapped his fingers against Rowan's throat. Rowan thanked him in the same manner and stepped back to my side. I wasn't sure if it was something I needed to do since I wasn't technically a shifter, but I *was* in this pack, and my husband was unequivocally our leader, so I too stepped forward and bared my throat to Phoenix.

His hand rose, but instead of tapping his fingers to my neck, he wrapped them around the back of my head and pulled me into a tight embrace. He buried his nose in my hair and inhaled a deep breath of my scent, which he'd told me smelled like a hundred wildflowers. Just as I was relaxing against his warm, strong body, Phoenix surprised me by hoisting me into his arms and throwing me over his shoulder.

"I need to reconnect with my mate," he told Rowan and Stone. I wished I could see their reactions, but I was also pleased with my face full of sexy Phoenix ass.

"What should we do with the bodies, Alpha?" Rowan asked.

"They broke all rules and protocols with their attack and don't deserve a proper burial," Phoenix replied. "Stone, collect the bodies and burn them. Rowan, perform a cleansing ritual on the earth."

"Yes, Alpha," they both answered.

Not gonna lie, hearing Phoenix take charge and give orders after seeing the proof of his raw power made me both proud and horny as hell. As Phoenix carried me toward our cabin, Stone and Rowan came into my line of vision. Rowan gave me a warm smile and Stone flashed two thumbs up before turning to take care of their tasks.

Chapter Twelve

Phoenix

My heart dropped at the sight of the shattered window as I carried Rory onto the porch of our cabin. My mate could have easily been killed tonight if he hadn't gotten away and called on his pack. I shook the thoughts from my head. Now wasn't the time to grieve over what *could* have happened. I'd replace the window later and clean up the glass shards so that Rory wouldn't get hurt. For now, I needed to spend time with my mate and hold him in my arms. I needed to feel him against me to prove he was safe.

I wanted nothing more than to take him into our bedroom and make love to him all night. I craved being as close as possible with him and strengthening our bond. But first, I needed to cleanse my skin of the blood and the scent of the shifters that attacked us. I carried Rory into the bathroom and placed him gently on his feet in front of me. I cupped his cheeks in my hands and gazed into his beautiful eyes.

"Thank you, sweetheart," I whispered before planting a sweet kiss on his lips.

Rory blinked in confusion. "For what?"

"For believing in me and reminding me what was important. Your strength and encouragement pushed me forward. I never could have won without you."

Rory shook his head. "Phoenix, you were incredible out there. You took on half the pack by yourself and you destroyed them!"

"Only because I was trying to get to you," I admitted. "Even though I knew Stone and Rowan would protect you, I lost control when I saw those men coming after you. Something snapped inside me and turned all of my fear and anger into aggression. I couldn't kill them fast enough. They were just obstacles in my way to get to you. But by the time I'd struck them down, the three of you had already taken care of the rest. When I saw you were okay, I could finally breathe again."

Rory reached up and ran his fingers through my scruffy beard. "And that makes you the best wolf husband in the world." I huffed a laugh and turned my head to place a kiss on the palm of his hand. "You always worry about me and take such good care of me. Tonight, I want you to let me take care of you."

Before I could ask what he meant, Rory stepped away towards the shower. He turned the dials and held his hand under the water to test the temperature. When he was satisfied, he folded his glasses on the sink and quickly removed his clothing. My mouth watered at the sight of his smooth, creamy skin. I wanted to sink my teeth into his neck and claim him as mine all over again.

"Not yet," Rory said with a smirk. I didn't have to ask his meaning, because his gaze was set on my dick, which was rapidly filling and rising. "First we need to get all of the dirt and blood off of you. It's making it hard for me to enjoy your scent."

I blinked in surprise as Rory led me into the shower. "You can scent me?"

He nodded. "At first, I thought it was your soap, but it doesn't smell anything like you. Then I thought it was your cologne, but you don't wear any. When you told me *I* had a natural scent, I figured out that you did too, and that I love it."

"What do I smell like?" I asked curiously. I couldn't pick up my own pheromones.

"Earth and evergreen," Rory smiled. "And it's incredible." He picked up a washcloth from a small shelf and wet it in the stream behind me before covering it with shower gel. He worked the soap up into a lather and touched the cloth to my chest. He cleansed my skin in small, gentle circles. "Does that feel okay?"

"It feels perfect." Everything about this moment was perfect; my mate's tender touch, the love in his eyes, and the way he was visually devouring my body.

"I'll never get over how sexy you are," Rory whispered. He scrubbed the cloth over my skin, trailing his fingers over the hills and valleys of my abdomen. "Or that you're all mine." He knelt before me and rubbed the washcloth down my leg. "I'm not pulling your hair, am I?"

"No, sweetheart." I smiled at the care he showed me; he'd just witnessed the destruction I was capable of, but still treated me with a tender touch. He saw past my alpha title and strong body and loved me for what was inside. Though he made it clear he appreciated the outside as well.

Rory gently scrubbed the mud and dried blood from my legs and feet. When I was fully clean, he dropped the washcloth on the floor of the shower and touched his hands to my shins. He swirled his fingers through the hair on my legs as they crept up over my knees and onto my thighs.

My eyes slid closed and I moaned as Rory cupped my heavy balls in his palm. He massaged my sensitive flesh and gently pulled my sack, sending a warm tingle prickling over my skin. "I love it when you touch me," I groaned as he wrapped his other hand around the base of my cock and slowly pulled from root to tip.

"I love touching you," he replied with another stroke, "But I want to try making you feel good another way." I peered down to find Rory staring at my firm cock, running his tongue along his bottom lip in the way that drove me wild.

Rory had never tasted me; we'd made love dozens of times over the past couple of weeks, but I was always ravenous for his body. I'd prep him and get inside him as quickly as possible, unable to stave off my desires.

Rory tore his eyes away from my dick and looked up at me with a question in his gaze. "Sweetheart, you never *have* to do anything for me," I told him, running my fingers through his damp hair, "But if it's something you *want* to do, I wish to experience everything with you."

"Me too." His gaze travelled back down my body, and I couldn't tear mine away from the sight of his tongue peeking out from between his lips. He touched it to the tip of my cock and licked away the drop of pre-cum brought there by his loving touch. Rory shuddered as the flavor hit his taste buds.

He swirled his tongue over my crown and lapped up every drop that leaked from me. My breath caught as he quickly flicked his tongue over my slit and Rory's eyes snapped up to my face.

"So good," I crooned, letting him know I loved his touch and that he was making me feel amazing. My lover was sometimes nervous when we tried new things, but everything he did to me felt wonderful. My words urged him on and Rory parted his lips to take my thick crown into his mouth.

He sucked against my tip and my knees threatened to buckle beneath me. I steadied myself with a hand to the shower wall as Rory slowly took in over half of my length. "That feels incredible," I breathed. My mate pushed forward, but gagged before all of my dick was down his throat. I pulled back a couple of inches and looked down in concern. "Are you okay?" Rory nodded as his cheeks reddened. "It's okay, sweetheart. Don't be embarrassed; you're doing so good. You don't have to try to take it all. Can I show you?" He nodded again.

I pulled my hips back until just my tip was between his lips and then pushed a few inches forward, gliding my length along his tongue. "Just like that," I moaned breathlessly as I pumped my hips back and forth, reveling in the feeling of his soft, warm throat around me. "Oh god, Rory, you feel so good."

He placed his hands flat against my hips to stop their movement and took over, bobbing his head back and forth. Every time he backed away, he swirled his tongue over my sensitive, leaking head. "Yes, sweetheart." My hand searched for purchase on the slippery wall as Rory sucked harder against me and nodded his head faster.

My pulse raced as I looked down at my mate. His full, pretty lips were stretched around my girth. His eyes were closed and his brow was furrowed in concentration as he sucked and milked my dick. "So beautiful," I moaned. Rory opened his eyes and looked up at me and I was caught off guard by the heat and determination in his gaze.

I knew I wasn't going to last when Rory trailed his hand down my thigh and gripped my balls again. He pulled and massaged my fuzzy orbs as he sucked me at a feverish pace. My sack jerked in his palm as my balls pulled up toward my body. "You're gonna make me come," I warned so that Rory would be prepared and not choke. My mate hummed and jerked his head back and forth even quicker. My balls rolled and I cried out as my dick swelled inside my lover's mouth.

I exploded, pumping stream after stream of my seed into Rory's eager throat. He swallowed quickly, drinking down every drop I gave him before milking my length with his fist and lapping up anything he may have missed.

Rory placed a sweet kiss on the tip of my softening dick and looked up at me again with wide eyes. My chest heaved as I tried to catch my breath after the brain scrambling orgasm he just pulled out of me. "You're incredible," I managed to get out. My mate's blinding grin threatened to take my breath away again.

I helped him onto his feet and ran my hands through his hair, slicking it back away from his face. "Now I want to make *you* feel incredible."

His gaze darkened and he nodded eagerly. "Please." It only took that one word to kick me into gear. I grabbed a bottle of lube from the shelf (we'd had sex in every room of our home and liked to be prepared) and poured a generous amount into my palm. I replaced the bottle and rubbed the slippery liquid between my hands.

I wrapped my fist around the base of his cock and my skin glided effortlessly over his as I pumped him in a steady rhythm. I squeezed firmly and jacked him in a corkscrew motion; exactly how I'd learned he liked it. Rory tipped his head back on his shoulders and moaned loudly as I stroked him.

"Baby, that feels so good."

I could make him feel even better. "Spread your legs for me, Rory." He did as I asked, pushing his feet to each side of the tub. I reached my free hand behind him and tickled down the crack of his ass. My lover moaned again as I brushed a slick fingertip across his hole. "You want it inside you?"

"Yes!" Rory steadied himself with a hand to the wall like I had as I pushed the tip of my finger through his ring of muscle.

"Mm, always so tight for me," I murmured, rocking my hand back and forth. I swirled my finger around, loosening his opening as I continued to jack his pretty dick. "Ready for another?" Rory bit down on his bottom lip and nodded. When I slid a second digit into his ass, he threw his head back and cried out at the ceiling. "You like that don't you?" His bottom lip found its way between his teeth again as he nodded quickly.

I loved the feeling of his tight, hot channel wrapped around my fingers, but I wanted to feel it wrapped around my cock. And thanks to shifter recovery time, I was hard and leaking again. "You want more? You want me to put my fat dick inside you?"

"Yes! *Please*, Phoenix, fuck me!"

I growled as I pulled my fingers free from his ass and dropped his dick from my hold. I gripped the backs of his thighs and hoisted him up into my arms. Rory wrapped his legs around my waist and I gripped the base of my dick. I lined my tip up with his hole and pushed inside.

Rory screamed as I popped through his tight ring and buried myself inside him. I stood still and steady, letting him adjust to my size. "Don't stop," he begged. "It's so good." I gripped his hips in my big hands and guided his body up and down, bouncing him on my cock.

Rory moaned each time my dick pierced deep between his cheeks. His passage squeezed around me, enveloping me in tight heat and incredible friction. My lover couldn't get enough. He reached behind him to flatten his palms against the wall and pushed against me as I thrust into him, burying me further inside him.

My girth rubbed against his inner walls as I impaled him, and I knew by the way he was chanting my name and drawing in ragged breaths I was pegging his prostate with each thrust.

"Please touch me," Rory asked with a wild look in his eye. My mate was desperate for release and I was desperate to give it to him. I released his hip and wrapped my hand around his dick once more. I pounded into his tight little ass and stroked him once, twice, three times and he erupted.

Warm cum splattered over my hand and onto Rory's stomach. I stroked him until nothing was left and he trembled in my arms. Then I wrapped my hand back around his hip and slammed him down onto my cock. Rory's eyes rolled back in his head as he enjoyed the aftershocks while I rode him hard and fast.

My orgasm started in my toes. They curled up and tingling heat shot up my calves and thighs, coming to rest in my balls. They lifted and rolled and I buried myself inside Rory's tight little asshole as I screamed out his name. My seed burst deep inside him and I couldn't help myself.

I leaned forward and sank my teeth into Rory's mating mark. He slapped the wall and yelled as his dick jerked and produced another powerful burst of cum that painted his balls and my stomach. My bite would always affect him this way, and it would never get old watching my mate come apart.

"Holy shit," Rory breathed after I retracted my teeth from his neck.

"My thoughts exactly."

After we caught our breath, I gently placed Rory on the floor and made sure his legs were steady before I let him go. Then I grabbed a fresh washcloth and lathered it up with body wash. Just as he'd done for me, I took my time carefully cleansing every inch of his body. Our lovemaking could get intense, but I wanted to make sure he always felt precious and cared for.

Once he was clean and rinsed, I helped him out onto the bath mat and dried his body. He dried me too and we stepped together over to the sink. We took turns brushing our teeth and I wrapped my arm around his shoulders, leading him into the bedroom.

"Come on, sweetheart; you've had a hard night. Let's get you to bed."

He nodded and started to climb into bed before abruptly turning around to face me. "Wait a minute, what about the window?"

"I'll get what I need to replace it tomorrow, but for tonight, I'll board it up once you're asleep."

"I can help."

I smiled and ran my fingers over his cheek. "I know you can, but you need your rest. I want to take care of you, and make sure our home is safe and comfortable for you."

Rory rose onto his tiptoes to give my lips a soft kiss. "You really are the best, you know that?"

"I know," I shrugged, making him laugh. I turned down the corner of the blankets and smiled as Rory climbed into bed, flinching when his tender ass rubbed against the sheets.

"Will you lay with me until I fall asleep?"

"Of course, sweetheart." I climbed into bed behind him and wrapped my arm around his thin waist.

"Let's try to make it more than two weeks before another terrifying, life-altering event takes place, okay? We've had quite enough of those."

I chuckled at my sweet mate and pulled him closer to me. "Deal."

He sighed and nestled his little naked ass against my groin. I could easily go for round three, but Rory *did* need his rest. I settled for kissing his neck and taking another deep breath of his intoxicating scent.

"I love you, Phoenix," Rory said before breaking out into a huge yawn.

"I love you too, Rory."

Within moments, my sweet, exhausted mate was snoozing in my arms.

Chapter Thirteen

Rory

I chuckled as I watched Phoenix fidget his fingers *again*. "You are a badass alpha wolf; why are you so nervous to meet my friend?" He and I were seated in the same pizza restaurant where I'd last seen Dax nearly a month ago waiting for him to arrive.

"Because he's very important to you. I know he's a big part of your life and I want him to like me."

My heart swelled at his words. He would never try and push Dax and me apart; he knew all of my love belonged to him and that Dax was just a very dear friend and family. Phoenix just wanted to be accepted and included in that friendship.

I buried my fingers in Phoenix's short beard and looked seriously into his eyes. "He's going to love you."

"How can you be so sure?"

"Because he'll see how much you love me." Phoenix's feelings for me were obvious, and that's what would matter to Dax. My husband smiled at me before pressing his lips against mine, kissing me slowly and tenderly, pouring his feelings into me.

"Oh, don't mind me," Dax's voice sounded from beside me. "It's not like I woke up early from sleeping after a midnight shift and drove across town to see you or anything. I'll just get my own table so you can ignore me in peace."

Phoenix ripped his lips from mine and gave Dax a wide-eyed look of panic. "I'm sorry, I didn't mean to be rude. I wasn't ignoring you on purpose."

I snorted a laugh and patted Phoenix's thigh. "It's okay, baby, he's just messing with you." I stood from the booth and faced Dax. "Hey, Da-" I didn't even get his whole name out (and it was a short name) before he pulled me into a tight hug.

"I missed you," he whispered to me, squeezing me tightly and rocking me back and forth.

"I missed you too." It was the longest amount of time we'd ever gone without seeing each other. We made no move to separate, and soon Phoenix stood from the booth as well to place his hand on the small of my back. He supported Dax's and my relationship, but that didn't mean he was happy about another man touching me for so long. I took the hint and stepped away from my friend. "Dax, this is Phoenix. Phoenix, this is my best friend Dax."

"Nice to meet you," Phoenix offered, holding out his hand. "I've heard so much about you."

"Same here," Dax said, shaking my husband's hand. "And I'm glad we're finally getting the chance to have a little chat." He gave Phoenix a serious look and pointed to the table. Phoenix swallowed hard before turning to sit back down.

When Phoenix's back was away from us, Dax looked at me with a huge, dumb grin and mouthed *'So hot'* to me. I nodded and mouthed back, *'I know, right?'* But by the time Dax took his seat across from Phoenix, he was all business again. I nestled in beside my husband and waited for the interrogation to begin.

"So, Phoenix," Dax began, crossing his thick arms over his chest and peering at my husband from under his brows, "What makes you think you're good enough for my Roar?" Phoenix flinched beside me at another man referring to me as his, but he didn't say anything. Hopefully he knew Dax was just trying to intimidate him and look out for me. He'd always thought of himself as my big brother (even though we were the same age) and was very protective over me.

"I know there's nothing I can do to ever deserve someone as wonderful as Rory," Phoenix replied. "But I thank Fate every day for giving him to me and I will spend my entire life loving him and taking care of him. I will support him and protect him all of my days."

Dax's jaw went slack and he blinked hard before shaking his head slightly, bringing back his unimpressed veneer. "I guess you don't sound *too* terrible," he shrugged. I scrubbed a hand over my mouth to keep from laughing; my friend was trying so hard. Dax leaned over the table toward Phoenix and added in a low voice, "But know this; if you *ever* hurt my friend, I'll make your life a living hell. I may not look like a threat, but I promise to make you beg for mercy, but I won't give it."

A slow smile spread across Phoenix's face as he turned to me. "I like him."

I smiled back and reached across the table to pat Dax's arm. "Yeah, me too."

After his warnings had been delivered, Dax warmed up to Phoenix quickly. We talked and laughed together as we scarfed down enough pizza and soda to feed six people instead of three. Phoenix had a high metabolism because he was a shifter, and mine was growing every day. Dax just really loved pizza, and I was happy to see him enjoying his meal without worrying about his body or what his terrible boyfriend might say. I *wasn't* happy with the way Dax kept yawning and rubbing his bloodshot eyes.

"You look so tired," I told him sadly. "I didn't mean to get you up so early after your shift."

"I was just teasing about that," he insisted with a wave of his hand. "I've actually got the night off, so I needed to get up or else I'd waste my first evening free from work in two weeks in bed."

"You haven't had a night off in two *weeks*?"

Dax yawned again as he shook his head. "I picked up some extra hours cleaning, plus the movie theater has been working me pretty regularly. With the two jobs, keeping house and cooking, I'm worn out."

"Maybe Justin could cook some meals so that you can rest," I suggested before I could stop myself. It never went well when I spoke against Justin, but thankfully Dax seemed too tired to get riled up.

"Well, it was part of our agreement when I moved in that I'd take care of the cooking and cleaning."

I gnashed my teeth together. I didn't know about this agreement; I would have fought harder against Dax moving out of our apartment if I had. Things made so much more sense now; Justin asked Dax to move in because he wanted a servant, not a boyfriend. The names Justin called him and the disgusted way he looked at him (not to mention the fact Dax said they hadn't been intimate in months) made me wonder if he even liked Dax, or just saw him as easy prey. Phoenix must have picked up on my irritation, because he put his warm palm on my thigh and patted gently, trying to calm me down.

"But I'm sure Justin will find work soon, so it'll get better," Dax insisted.

"Is he even *trying* to look for a job?" I snapped.

"I said he was," Dax bit back.

Shit. I knew that tone and Dax was about to blow his top. "Okay," I backed off, raising my hands in surrender. "I'm sorry, I didn't mean to accuse him of anything." That was a load of bullshit, but I didn't want to fight.

Dax scrubbed a hand over his face. "I'm sorry too. I'm just cranky because I'm so tired." He reached across the table and took my hand. "And because I've missed you. We haven't got to spend any time together; let's not spend what we *do* have fighting."

I squeezed his hand in agreement. "Hey, when's your next day off?"

"As long as they don't give me extra hours on this upcoming schedule, I'm off next Friday night."

"Why don't you come visit us?" I asked, looking between Dax and Phoenix. My husband smiled and nodded. "Take some time for yourself and come hang out and see our place. We'll order in food and you can meet the rest of our friends. Maybe we can even have a game night like we used to. How does that sound?"

"It sounds amazing," Dax grinned. My pulse raced at the idea of getting everyone together and having fun. "Can Justin come too?"

Fuuuuuuuck. Well, we can forget about the 'fun' part. "Of course," I choked out.

"Great! Well, speaking of Justin, I'd better get home to him. I haven't spent much time with him either and he may want to do something together this evening." I doubted it; Justin never seemed to want to go anywhere in public with Dax.

"Okay. Well, I'm glad you guys finally got to meet," I replied, motioning between him and Phoenix. "And I'm really looking forward to next Friday." And really hoping that Justin caught the plague or something equally as terrible and had to stay home. To suffer. Alone. The thought brought a warm smile to my face.

"Me too," Dax smiled back, though I sincerely doubted it was for the same reason. "Oh shit, my brain is all over the place." He leaned up on one hip to grab his wallet out of his back pocket. "I almost ran out of here without paying."

"It's my treat," Phoenix insisted.

Dax smiled wider and replaced his wallet. "Thank you." He stuck his hand out and Phoenix gave it a firm shake. "It was great to meet you." He stood up out of the booth and leaned over to give me one more hug. "Be good to him," he said, looking at

Phoenix when he stood back up. "He's the best."

"Yes he is," Phoenix agreed. Dax waved goodbye and disappeared out the front entrance. My husband looked to me wearing a sad smile. "You okay?"

"Not really." I told him more about Justin and Dax's relationship, and how I was afraid my friend was being mistreated. I explained my fears of Dax being used for money, chores and food, and that he wasn't being loved or cherished. "Now that I'm in a relationship, I see how terrible his really is."

"I'm sorry, sweetheart." Phoenix placed a gentle kiss to my temple. "I know it's hard because you want to support your friend but also don't want to upset him." He let out a long sigh. "Maybe if he spends more time with us, he'll see what it looks like to have an incredible man."

"You *are* pretty great," I told him seriously.

"I was talking about you."

My heart skipped a beat and I placed a tender kiss to his lips. "How about you take me home and we can make each other *feel* incredible?" Phoenix let out a low growl in agreement. "God, I'll never get tired of that." My husband threw a few twenty dollar bills onto the table before I practically pulled him out of the booth and dragged him out to the truck.

*****

Phoenix pulled into the dirt spot next to our cabin and I jumped out of the truck cab, eager to get inside and love on my man.

"Hey, guys!" Rowan shouted from his seat on his porch.

I was *really* not in the mood to stop and have a conversation, or have to explain, 'Sorry, can't talk; we're on our way to fuck', although I was positive he'd understand. Hoping to find some middle ground, I raised my hand over my head and waved. When I did, Rowan's head tipped to the side and he sniffed the breeze. He leapt from his chair and over his porch railing and sprinted over until he was right in front of me. Phoenix gave him a curious look as he walked around the trunk and stood by my side.

Rowan paid him no attention. Instead, he gripped my shoulders and eagerly sniffed my neck before plastering his face on my chest and breathing deeply.

"What the hell do you think you're doing?" Phoenix growled and pushed Rowan away with a firm shove. Rowan captured Phoenix's hand and brought it to his face, thoroughly sniffing it as well.

"You're both carrying a scent," Rowan explained excitedly. "It's stronger on Rory; it's all over the front of his body, but it's just on your hand. Where were you? Who were you with? Did you both touch the same person?" His eyes frantically shifted between the two of us as he fired off the questions.

"We went to town to meet with my friend Dax. I hugged him and Phoenix shook his hand," I explained, hope barreling through my chest as puzzle pieces fell into place.

"Dax," Rowan repeated on a whisper. A dreamy smile crossed his lips and his eyes glistened. He swallowed hard before standing up straight and announcing proudly, "Dax is my mate."

The End

Thank you for reading *Pine Ridge Pack Book 1: Mine to Save.* If you enjoyed the book, please consider leaving a review, and stay tuned for Dax and Rowan's story in the next book in the series, *Pine Ridge Pack Book 2: Mine to Keep*, available now!

Other Reads (Free with Kindle Unlimited):

M/M Paranormal Romance:

Once Bitten: Javier Coven Book 1
(Vampire M/M)

Twice Shy: Javier Coven Book 2
(Vampire M/M)

Twice Bitten: Javier Coven Book 3
(Vampire M/M/M)

Untitled: Duff Coven Book 1 (Vampire
M/M) Coming soon!

Mine to Save: Pine Ridge Pack Book 1
(M/M Wolf Shifter)

Mine to Keep: Pine Ridge Pack Book 2
(M/M Wolf Shifter)

Mine to Protect: Pine Ridge Pack Book 3
(M/M Wolf Shifter) Coming soon!

Shadow Walker: Bay City Coven Book 1
(Vampire M/M)

Into the Shadows: Bay City Coven Book 2 (Vampire M/M) Coming soon!

Magic Touch (M/M Mage)

<u>M/M Series:</u>

Arrested Hearts Book 1: Gage & Tyson (M/M) *Can be read as standalone

Arrested Hearts Book 2: Chris & Lyle (M/M)

Arrested Hearts Book 3: Mike & Jonah (M/M)

Arrested Hearts Book 4: Sam & Jordan (M/M) Coming soon!

My Everything (M/M) *Can be read as standalone

My Forever (novella sequel to "My Everything") (M/M)

Head Over Wheels (M/M) *Can be read as standalone

Head Over Wheels: Book 2 (M/M)

Care for You (Head Over Wheels: Book 3) (M/M)

My Grumpy Old Bear (Loveable Grumps: Book 1) *Can be read as standalone

My Confused Cub (Lovable Grumps: Book 2) Coming soon!

Beautiful Dreamer (M/M Age Play) (Secret Desires: Book 1) *Can be read as standalone

Lost Boy (M/M BDSM) (Secret Desires: Book 2) Coming soon!

M/M Standalone

Ours to Love (M/M/M)

Chasing Jackson (M/M)

Nervous Nate (M/M Age Play Romance)

Valentine Shmalentine (M/M)

M/F Series:

Housewife Chronicles: Complete Series
(M/F)

Luscious: Complete Series (M/F)

Made in the USA
Coppell, TX
22 June 2021

57862983R10184